By Fay Risner

Enjoy
Fay Risner

ISBN 1438248202
EAN 13 9781438248202

Publisher Create Space

Booksbyfay
http://www.booksbyfay.tripod.com

1

This book is dedicated to Edna Heitmann, my writing teacher. She taught me, edited my writing and gave me advice on how to make my stories better. I thank her for her encouragement that helped me keep trying to write.

Specious Nephew

Chapter 1

God didn't intend for old folks to like fall, thought Gracie Evans as she vigorously rubbed her aching, left knee. She listened to the crisp, north breeze rattle brown leaves on the unkempt, pivot hedge along side of Moser Mansion Rest Home For Women. A shiver run through Gracie, settling in under the dark gray braids wrapped around her head.

In an instant, a strong gust of wind tore loose a handful of dry leaves and scooted them along the porch floor in front of Gracie and her companion, Melinda Applegate. The leaves made it all the way to the south end of the porch, swirled up in a whirlwind motion then scattered across the yard, lodging in the dead leaf piles at the base of the hedge and the picket fence.

Looking at the clematis on the trellis in front of her, Gracie grimaced. The look of it was more proof that fall was an ugly time of year. It was the ninth of September. The vine had thinned to a screen of yellow leaves, like what was left of the ones on the honeysuckle and morning glory vines that grew on either end of the porch.

Not that Gracie needed shade from the hot, summer sun now. The two handmade, Amish rockers positioned behind each of the three vines no longer needed protection. In fact, what little warmth the sun provided soaked into her, feeling mighty good now that this sudden cool snap hinted at an early frost.

She didn't bother to squint through the peek holes in the

vines. She kept them clear of leaves during the summer to give Melinda and her an unobstructed view of the neighbors comings and goings. Now there were more natural openings then leaves, and wouldn't you know not much exciting to watch across the street since the lady of the evening, Rachel Simpson, was murdered and her house burnt to the ground.

Two doors north of Rachel's house, Mavis and Dan Jordan split up during the summer. That couple sure kept things exciting in the neighborhood for awhile with their fighting. Many a night she watched Dan Jordan sneak into the side door of Rachel Simpson's house after dark until his wife, Mavis, found out. Then Dan ran off. After that, Mavis went off the deep end. She murdered the Simpson girl, realized that Gracie and Melinda knew too much and put fear into everyone at the Moser mansion until Gracie and Melinda helped get Mavis arrested for Rachel's murder. Now the Jordan house stood empty.

A retired couple, Earl and Sara Bullock, owned the house on the middle lot across the street. Nice enough couple but about as exciting as watching an old dog chase his tail. The highlight of their day seemed to be working in the flower beds and garden in the summer. Of course, that was more than she had to keep her busy. Gracie had to give them that. All she did was sit and let people wait on her.

Now with fall coming on, Gracie expected the Bullocks would stay out of sight, indoors by the fire, but this day had certainly been different. There had been a flurry of activity at their house. For the better part of the day, Gracie sit tight in her rocker, trying to figure out what the heck was happening over there.

The fact was there just wasn't any other way for Gracie to occupy her time in the rest home. She was willing to stick with sitting on the Moser porch until much colder weather hit Locked Rock, Iowa to keep from sitting closed away in the dark parlor. That would happen soon enough. Of course, Melinda agreed to rock on the porch with her. That helped. They always had each other to pass the time of day with. That is, when she could keep Melinda awake.

If there happened to be any tidbits of Sara's conversation that Gracie missed, she could always count on Sara to fill her in when their neighbor came to visit.

Besides Gracie reasoned, there wasn't anything wrong with a body being curious. Gracie felt she needed to stay informed about what was happening in the community. What easier way to do it for an old person besides listening and watching the neighbors.

"A penny for your thoughts," suggested Melinda in her soft voice, breaking the silence. She relaxed her head against her rocker. Her light gray, curls flattened to her face like tiny springs. The petite woman gave Gracie a long, thoughtful look.

Gracie studied on what she should say before she spoke, wanting to blurt out that God hadn't intended for fall to be a season suitable for old folks, but she resisted. Melinda would scold her for being sacrilegious if she bothered to be so truthful.

Instead, she looked down at the sunlight that filtered through the vine onto her lap. Stretching a crooked finger out, she tapped at the pale yellow sparkles of light that danced along the folds of her brown skirt. Finally, she answered in her brassy voice, waving her finger back and forth toward the open space between the two vines. "I'm thinking now that the sun's peeking under the roof we should move our rockers over so we get the full sunshine. I don't know about you, but I'm mighty chilly. Here it is early in the afternoon when the day should be the warmest. If you ask me it's too early to have this cold a weather."

Melinda smiled at Gracie's complaining. She replied softly, "Well, you know the old saying. If you don't like the weather in Iowa, wait awhile. It'll change."

"Just the same, I'd rather not freeze to death any sooner than I have to. A body could catch her death sitting in the shade on a day like today. Let's move over in the sunlight."

Melinda nodded agreement. She rose, scooted her rocker over, and left room for Gracie. Tugging her rocker into position, Gracie plopped down next to Melinda. Tapping her toes on the floor, she rocked energetically, hoping that would help warm her up.

A group of children ran down the street, shouting and laughing. *Definitely the fall season is for the younger generations,* confirmed Gracie to herself. Young ones stayed active enough that they didn't feel the chill in the air. Thank goodness her mind was clear enough that she remembered those days, but she gave a deep sigh when she thought about how long ago that was.

Gracie contemplated Main Street with hitching racks almost empty of buggies and horses. "Not much business at the stores with the farmers in the fields, gathering in the corn crops before the first snow comes. Orie Lang hadn't even been by much lately to take Miss Molly for a buggy ride."

"He managed to stop picking corn long enough to pick Miss Molly up for church again Sunday. Most times he stays for dinner like last Sunday before he heads back to the farm," defended Melinda.

"Expect Aunt Pearlbee's cooking is the only good meal that bachelor gets. He's no dummy," replied Gracie.

Smiling, Melinda made a tent of her fingers and

brought them up to touch her lips. "If you'd been paying attention lately, you'd notice Mr. Orie isn't taking notice of Aunt Pearlbee's cooking while he's here."

"Come to think of it, Mr. Orie didn't seem in such a hurry last Sunday. He spent a good part of the afternoon in the parlor with Miss Molly. He must be about done with the harvest," decided Gracie.

"Reckon so. It'll be good for Miss Molly when Mr. Orie starts coming more regular. Since they've been sparking, Miss Molly seems so happy," said Melinda.

Gracie didn't have a reply for that comment so she sat quietly drifting in her thoughts. She watched a couple of squirrels, chasing each other along side the porch. For the last several days, they scampered across the yard with their cheeks full. Now that their fur coats had grown thick and fuzzy to ward against the cold, they sensed it was time to store a food supply for the winter. They buried walnuts and acorns in the ground or hid their bootee at the base of the hedge.

It seemed like only yesterday, Melinda and she watched from the gazebo while a couple of squirrels scurried up the old maple in the backyard, carrying food to babies in a leafy nest. *It must be true that the time passes faster as a body gets older. No doubt about it,* thought Gracie, frowning. She looked at the brown spots covering the back of her hands and wondered when they had turned ugly on her.

In her younger days, she didn't have time to worry about yesterday or tomorrow for that matter. In the fall, she kept busy on her farm. Just like the men farmers, she worked along side a wagon pulled by a team of work horses. She yanked the ears out of the dried shucks and threw them at the wagon. As she walked down the rows between the dried stalks, she shouted, "Come Queen, come Buck." The horses moved

7

slowly past her, stopping when Gracie hollered whoa. All the while hurrying as fast as she could, Gracie worked to fill the wagon, making the most of the daylight hours. She was pretty darn good at picking corn. As good as any man she knew.

And now what am I gathering? She asked herself at that moment in 1903 while she sat on the mansion porch in Locked Rock, Iowa. A sudden breeze blowing from Canada made her mighty uncomfortable. Gracie silently answered her question with, *goose bumps.* She vigorously rubbed her arms. Tugging her walnut stained, knit shawl tighter over the front of her long sleeve, tan blouse, she smoothed it out in her lap over her dark brown, calico skirt.

What she needed was something to think about besides being cold like what was going on in the front yard right then. A swarm of monarch butterflies fluttered across the lawn, flitting from the large rest home sign over to the vines then back to the picket fence. They seemed restless as if too tired to light and rest. The orange and black blurs soared up high and floated down in a slow, graceful ballet. Migrating on their journey south, the butterflies needed to rest for a spell, but by morning, they would be on their way again.

Once in awhile in the summer, a lonely butterfly flitted around the honeysuckle, but that wasn't the same kind of excitement for Gracie. It would be another year before a large number flocked together to give this kind of show and then only for a few hours on their way south.

As the monarchs fluttered down the street, Gracie relaxed back against her rocker and sighed.

"Gracie, if you keep frowning, you're face is going to freeze that way with as cool as it's getting," teased Melinda. "What's the matter with you today?"

"I hate the cold of fall and winter. That's all. I feel

winter coming in my bones already, and I dread it," Gracie said with sincerity.

"Well, worrying about something that you can't stop from happening isn't going to make you feel any better. I swear the better I get to know you the more the word curmudgeon comes to mind." The way Melinda looked at Gracie wasn't altogether flattering.

Gracie gave her a hard look right back. "Whoa there! That don't sound like a nice thing to call me. What is this crud mudge on anyway?"

"The word is curmudgeon. If you want to know what it means look it up in the dictionary in the Moser library," said Melinda.

"Fine friend you are. Calling me names," snapped Gracie, wiggling indignantly in her rocker.

The screen door hinges squeaked. The cook, Pearlbee, shuffled slowly through the doorway, steadying a tray with two cups on it. The thought ran through Gracie's mind that if Pearlbee's hips got any broader, she'd have to turn sideways to go through the doors. Wouldn't do to bring that up to the cook though. Let Pearlbee's dander get up and she turned into a cyclone in action.

"Hi, Pearlbee," greeted Gracie. "Didn't realize it was tea time yet. We can sure use that."

"Yes, thank you, Aunt Pearlbee. I'm so glad Miss Molly decided to start having tea time. It breaks up the afternoon." Pearlbee lowered the tray down to Melinda. She hooked her fingers in the handle of a steaming cup, lifted it off the tray and wrapped her hands around it.

"I'm sure ready for something to warm me up," said Gracie, reaching for her steaming cup.

The cook's unsteady gait made it hard for her to keep

9

the tray from wavering. Melinda suggested in concern for the cook's safety, "Aunt Pearlbee, you really should use your cane more."

"Ah's knowed it Missus, but cain't when I gets my hands full," declared Pearlbee.

"Maybe we should come get our own tea from now on. That would be of help, wouldn't it, Gracie?" suggested Melinda.

Gracie thought Pearlbee puffed up some. Never could tell when she'd get miffed about someone taking a chore away from her. Gracie sure didn't want that anger directed at her. Let this be Melinda's idea. Noncommittally, she shrugged her shoulders. "Don't make no never mind to me."

"Then that's what we'll do. You just let us know when you're ready Aunt Pearlbee. From now on, we'll come to the kitchen after the tea." As if she sensed Pearlbee might not know how to take this helping hand, Melinda gave the cook a close inspection and quickly changed the subject to one favorable to Pearlbee. "My, you do look nice in your new uniform, Aunt Pearlbee," she complimented.

"Thank ya, Missus," beamed Pearlbee, swishing her hips exaggeratedly to model the full effect of her newly acquired, black, challis dress set off by a white linen collar and cuffs on the long sleeves. Pearlbee reached for the hem of her full length, stiffly starched, white apron and held it out. She twisted around to show them the fancy way the pointed yoke straps came to a v in back where the ties made a bow.

Gracie took a sip from her cup before she watched the cook model her uniform. Drinking the warm tea make her even more uncomfortable. "Pearlbee, find us those quilts we cover our laps with when you have time. I don't think it's going to warm up enough out here this afternoon to be comfortable without them."

"Sure thing, Miss Gracie. Ah's be right back." Pearlbee waddled back to the screen door, balancing the empty tray.

Melinda watched the cook disappear then chastised, "Gracie, the least you could have done was tell Aunt Pearlbee you liked her new uniform."

Gracie pursed her lips, thinking about her answer. "Maybe but she looked all right in the ever day outfits she used to wear as far as I'm concerned."

"But she's proud of that uniform, and she does look nice in it," insisted Melinda.

"Don't expect Pearlbee would have gotten that fancy getup if she hadn't kept up such a fuss over that missing red apron we borrowed and didn't bring back. Miss Molly just gave her the uniform to calm her down," reminded Gracie, looking away from Melinda to across the street. Her mind was torn between arguing with Melinda and wondering what the two strange men were up to at the Bullocks. They made repeated trips, carrying boards and rolls of wiring into the house.

"What do you mean *we?*" Melinda's sweet, quiet voice rose a little. She darted a glance at the door. Focusing on Gracie, she lowered her voice, "As I remember it, that idea was yours, putting the apron in the package mean Mavis hid in exchange for the bloody dress she wore when she murdered Rachel Simpson. You're just lucky Aunt Pearlbee hasn't found out yet."

Gracie straightened in her rocker, squared her shoulders and jabbed a crooked finger at Melinda. "I'm lucky? As I recall you were right there in the tool shed in the middle of the night helping me find that package. Weren't you?"

Melinda sunk back in her rocker. "You're right," she

11

muttered half heartily, looking down at her folded hands in her lap.

A door bang across the street. Gracie put her attention in that direction. She sure didn't want to miss anything. With curiosity in her voice, she exclaimed, "There comes a couple men out of Sara Bullock's house again. Wonder what she's having done? Sure was a mess of boards and wire, those men unloaded from that wagon this morning."

"Look at that fence post those two men put up in the corner of the yard. Must be all of thirty feet tall. Makes me nervous wondering what kind of animal Earl intends to keep in Rachel Simpson's yard when they get it fenced in," said Melinda.

"That ain't a fence post. No animal needs a fence that high in the air," snorted Gracie in disdain. "That's a city girl for you."

"Well, Miss Know It All, what is it for then? Oh wait, here comes Sara. We'll just ask her," returned Melinda, defensively.

"Yahoo, ladies," shouted Sara, waving at them.

Gracie noted under her breath, "Sara, got her apron on. Must be making a hurry up call."

Melinda returned the wave and called eagerly, "Good afternoon. Come on up here."

Sara settled her wide hips between the arms of a rocker behind the honeysuckle vine. She untied her bonnet and removed it from her head.

Anxious to get out of Sara what was going on, Melinda asked, "We've been dying of curiosity about all the activity at your place. What you fixing?"

Gracie leaned forward to look around Melinda.

Sara took her time folding and placing her bonnet in her

lap. She knew the elderly women could hardly wait to satisfy their curiosity. Grinning, she said, "Not fixing anything. I got me a job. That stuff goes with it."

"What kind of job?" Rushed out of Gracie's mouth.

"I'm a telephone switch board operator," informed Sara proudly.

"What's a telephone?" Gracie wanted to know.

"That's one of those new contraptions that people are talking on to each other now," shared Sara.

"Well, what is that big fence pole in the corner of your yard for?" quizzed Melinda.

Sara giggled. "It's not a fence pole. That's a telephone pole."

"See there," Gracie rubbed in. "I told you that was no fence post."

"Let Sara finishing tell us what it is then," Melinda snipped peevishly.

Their neighbor continued to explain, "There will be more poles set down the block. Wire has to be strung on them and hooked to the houses of everyone who has a telephone to send messages over."

"What's going on out here?" Molly Moser peeked through the screen door. "I thought I heard talking."

"Afternoon, Molly. I was just telling Gracie and Melinda about my new job," replied Sara.

"What! You have a job? Tell me, too." Molly popped outside. The screen door shut with a hollow bang and bounced a couple times before it stilled. The young woman scurried over to sit down in the rocker next to Sara. She gripped the rocker seat, leaned forward and put all her attention on their neighbor.

"I'm going to run the switchboard for the telephones

out of my home. I'm what they call a switchboard operator," Sara announced proudly. "Want to come see what it looks like? The workmen should have everything about set up by now."

"Sure, I'd like to see," said Molly, eagerly.

Melinda looked at Gracie. "We want to go, too. Don't we?"

"Reckon." With very little enthusiasm, Gracie tried to digest what this new gadget that Sara described was all about as they crossed the street. She wasn't so sure she was going to like whatever it turned out to be.

The small, clapboard house the Bullocks owned was one of several look alike houses in town built in a hurry to accommodate people that moved to town after the railroad came. Gracie followed behind Molly and Melinda through the neat, but sparse parlor. Between the worn, dark brown, horsehair couch and a stuffed chair that matched it sat a table with a kerosene lamp in the middle surrounded by books. A rocker was by the front window. Near it sat a small table with a bouquet of pink and lavender asters in the center. Most likely they'd be the last flowers Sara would gather this year out of her flower beds.

The middle of the floor was covered by a large, oval, multicolored rag rug. Knowing how handy Sara was, Gracie figured she braided it from sewing scraps and the best parts of old clothes. Sara like Gracie never threw anything away. Gracie's mother used to say, "Just as sure as shootin' you throw away something, there'll come the day you could have used it." Over the years, Gracie found her mother's advice to be right. What never came up was the fact that finding something later that had been laid back for future use was often a hopeless case. In later years, Gracie hunted through the piles of objects discarded by her parents and herself, searching for an item. If it took very long to find what she was looking for, she'd have to stop and think a while to remember why she wanted to find the object in the first place.

Sara motioned for her guests to follow her. She led them to a door on the north end of the parlor. "This is the spare bedroom, but there's room for the bed and the switchboard, too."

When they heard the women, the two workers, in chambray work shirts and jeans, got up from a kneeling position. Both of them were covered in dirt and sawdust. They had stuffed a vast number of rubber coated wires attached to the back of the switchboard into a hole in the board floor. The men stepped back from the large piece of plywood nailed in one corner to let Sara and her friends view their handiwork.

"We just about have the switchboard hooked up, Mrs. Bullock. You'll be able to try it out afore long," the taller of the two men told Sara, pointing to the board full of small, gold cranks with white knobs.

Gracie leaned forward to inspect the silver plates below the cranks. She recognized several names. Sara stepped up beside her and picked up a brown, bell shaped piece resting on a small wooden platform at the edge of the switchboard. "This is called a receiver. It's what I listen into when folks talk to me." She held it to her ear and pointed to a wooden framed hole at the side of the switchboard. "This is what I talk into."

"Who all has one of these telephones?" Molly asked..

"The Locked Rock Mercantile and some of the other businesses. Some folks in town like Doc Lawson, Madge Potter, Phillip Harris, and a few others," said Sara. "Not many people yet, but more will want one once they see how it works."

"Sounds like folks that has money to me. I'll bet

15

something like this gadget don't come cheap. What good is it going to be when no one that we want to talk to has one of them," said Gracie in a matter of fact tone.

Ignoring Gracie, Melinda asked, "How far away can you talk on one of these things?"

"To anyone that has a telephone all over the country. Lots of folks have them out east in the bigger cities like New York."

Molly studied the switchboard. Suddenly, she spoke. "I'd like to have one, too."

"Really, Miss Molly," said Melinda, gleefully.

"Yes, think how quick it'd be to get Doctor Lawson if one of us needs him. All we'd have to do is ring him up. Can you sign me up, Sara?"

"I sure can. You'll have one put in tomorrow."

"Golly Moses, that soon. I'm excited about this. Aren't you ladies?" Instantly, her thoughts turned elsewhere. Molly glanced down at the watch attached to her blouse. "Oh my, look at the time. We better think about heading home. Aunt Pearlbee must have dinner about ready, and she doesn't like it if her food gets cold."

Chapter 2

During supper, Gracie watched Molly from across the table. The young woman hadn't touch a bit of the fried chicken and mash potatoes on her plate. In fact for some reason, she was doing an uncommon amount of fidgeting. Molly unfolded the blue linen napkin and stretched it out on her lap. As if that didn't suit, she picked the napkin up and refolded it to a smaller size. Running a finger along the folded edge of the napkin, she made new creases in the fabric. Holding it in her hands a moment, she seemingly rethought what she needed to do and decided to use the napkin for what it was intended. she shook it out and spread it back over her lap. All the while, her plate full of food was getting cold.

Gracie watched for awhile before she poked Melinda in the ribs with one of her crooked fingers. Melinda stopped eating and looked down to see what had stuck her in the side. Wordlessly, she raised an eyebrow questioningly in Gracie's direction. Gracie turned her gnarled finger under the table toward Molly.

Melinda looked over at the younger woman and watched her fidget for a moment. "Miss Molly, are you not feeling well, dear?"

"I'm fine, Miss Melinda. Just dandy. What would make you say a thing like that," chanted Molly. Snatching the napkin off her lap, she dropped it in a heap on the table beside her plate. She ran her fingers through her honey colored hair, picked up her fork and nibbled at the cold potatoes as if that should end of the subject.

"You really don't look too well. That's why. Rather pale and -- well -- nervous," insisted Melinda.

That got Libby and Moxie's attention. They looked in Molly's direction, puzzled by the conversation. They had been too busy eating to notice Molly acting nervous.

"Oh, that. I'm fine. It's just that I have something to tell all of you. An announcement if you will. Aunt Pearlbee, come sit with us. I might as well tell everyone at the same time," Molly said with a giggle.

With a look of surprise on her face at being included at the table during mealtime, Pearlbee flopped down in a chair next to Moxie.

"Now we're listening," said Gracie. "Get on with it."

Molly licked her lips and took a deep breath. "I wanted to wait for Orie to come in tonight before I told you this, but I can't wait any longer. Golly Moses, I'm about to bust at the seams. Orie has asked me to marry him," rushed out of the young woman's mouth.

"That's wonderful," cried Melinda, clasping her hands together.

"That's great," said Libby quietly with a slight smile.

"I'm thinking this be super news, Molly. We're all very happy for ye. Congratulations," expelled Moxie. Jumping up, she threw her arms around Molly and gave her a hug.

Molly gave Gracie a tentative look. "Miss Gracie, you're very quiet. What do you think of my news?

"It's about time," she cracked. Then she grinned. The young woman looked a little more relaxed now that she had confessed what was bothering her.

"When is the wedding going to be?" asked Melinda, excitedly.

"Orie says he'd like it to be as soon as possible. I tend

to agree. After all, it's not as if we're youngsters and would be expected to have a long engagement. What do you ladies think?"

"For sure, I agree whole heartily," concurred Moxie, blinking her eyes at Molly.

"We're thinking about an October wedding. That means a lot of quick planning has to be done and carried out in the next six weeks. I think it should be warm enough yet in October to have a wedding outside in the gazebo."

"A garden wedding. How wonderful," clapped Melinda.

"I'm going to need all of you to help me so I was wondering if we could all get together in the parlor this evening. Aunt Pearlbee I'd like you to go fetch Uncle Malachi. After Orie gets done out at the farm, he's coming in so we can get started on arrangements. Will you all help me?" Molly asked as she looked around the table.

"Yes," the other women said in unison.

"Each of you should be thinking of a relative or friend that you'd like to invite to the wedding to spend the day with you. I'm going to have the invitations printed up at the newspaper office. I'll need help addressing the envelopes after we decide on the guest list. Be sure and give me your guest's name and address."

Melinda had the saddest look on her face. Gracie couldn't figure out what was the matter with her. First she bubbled like a spring flowing out of the ground. Now she seemed about ready to bawl. One thing was for sure, Gracie wasn't about to point Melinda's emotional status out with Molly so lighthearted.

The kerosene lamp in the middle of the table glowed, reflecting in Molly's hazel eyes, generating a gleam of happiness over everyone at the table. *It's nice to see her so*

19

happy after all those years of being an old maid, thought Gracie. It was a wonderful thing that the fellow Molly was marrying was the man she wanted all along. Funny how life works out. If Molly's mother, Nora, hadn't interfered years before and sent Molly off to boarding school, she'd have been Mrs. Orie Lang a long time ago.

That evening, the women waited in the parlor for Orie to show up. Everyone sat in their usual spots. Molly and Moxie chose the dark blue, velvet settee in the middle of the room. Gracie and Melinda sat in the stuffed, dark blue chairs across from the settee. Libby always sat in the French Victorian chair in the far corner next to the small, reading table. That spot was segregated from the rest of the room so Libby could read in the yellow circle of light from the lamp above her and not be bothered by conversation from the others. Exceptions that night were Pearlbee and her husband, Malachi, standing by the door. The couple bowed their snow white heads, looking uncomfortable at being included in this gathering.

"Golly Moses, please sit down, Aunt Pearlbee and Uncle Malachi. You can't stand forever. This may be a long evening," said Molly. She laughed heartily as she motioned them to come closer.

Aunt Pearlbee's cane thudded on the floor as she shuffled over to the piano stool. She plopped down and smoothed the wrinkles out her new, white apron. Malachi sat slowly down on one of the two Victorian chairs by the fireplace as if the dainty chair would collapse under his weight. Atop skinny, curved legs, the chair's oval back and square seat was upholstered in light blue fabric adorned with a large, white calla lily cupped by embroidered green leaves.

Gracie knew just how Malachi felt. She'd never cared for fancy chairs. In her opinion, they were more for looking at then sitting on so what good were they? Her farmhouse had been full of handmade wooden furniture made by her father, rough looking for sure but sturdy and serviceable. Her renters, the Sawyer family, were enjoying her father's handiwork and glad to have furniture that would last them for years.

"First, Moxie I'd like to ask you if you'd be my bridesmaid," asked Molly.

"Sure and it would be my pleasure," answered Moxie, gleefully.

"Hello! Anybody home?" Orie yelled from down the hall.

"Of course, we are. Come into the parlor," Molly twisted on the settee toward the door and called back.

"Well, have you told them our news?" Orie asked from the doorway. He checked out the pleased grins on everyone's face and ducked his head bashfully. "I reckon you have from the looks I'm getting."

"Yes," Molly said with a hardy laugh. "They wormed it out of me. I'm sorry I didn't wait so we could tell them together. But now come sit with us," Molly said, patting the empty space Moxie had made between Molly and her on the settee. "We have a wedding to plan and fast. I've asked everyone to help us. I just asked Moxie to be my bridesmaid. Orie, you'll have to pick a best man."

"Already have. Earl Bullock."

"Wonderful choice. I'll ask Sara to be in charge of the reception so she won't feel left out." Molly smiled at the cook and then at the handyman. "Now Aunt Pearlbee and Uncle Malachi, I'd like to ask you to give me away."

"Yes ma'am, we's be honored," assented Pearlbee in a husky voice.

"Ah thinks that's mighty fine," agreed Malachi, smiling

at Molly like a proud father.

"Are you sure that's such a good idea, Miss Molly?" Libby looked from Malachi to Pearlbee and back to Molly, frowning. "I mean ... well .. ." She licked her lips, trying to figure out how she should phrase what she was thinking. "Having the cook and handyman give the bride away isn't usually what's done." Libby looked around for help from the other ladies, but none of them said anything.

"Miss Libby, I've never been one to conform to what others do. You should know that by now. If Orie is agreeable?" She looked at him for approval. He nodded yes. "and he is so that's all that matters to me."

Pearlbee gave Molly a worried look. "Missus, the lady might be right. Ya wants to make
sure everything goes all right for yer wedding. That's whats me and Malachi wants. That's important to us."

"Well, what's important to me is the two of you are like second parents to me. You were always here for me. You took care of me more than my parents did when I was growing up. Seemed like they were always off on one of those long trips."

"Yes ma'am, reckon we took good care of ya, and enjoyed ever minute of it too," exclaimed Pearlbee.

"I'm glad, because I don't know what I'd have done without you two dear people," Molly said. She got up throw her arms around Pearlbee then went to Malachi to give him a hug. Rubbing her hands together, she sat back down on the settee. "Now on with the planning. Orie, I've decided I'd like to have the ceremony in the gazebo.

"What if it rains," worried Melinda. "Don't you think you should use the church?"

"No, I really want the wedding outdoors in the sunshine, surrounded by my family and friends. If it's a rainy day, we can have the ceremony in front of the winding staircase. The guests can be seated in the dining room, but I really hope that doesn't happen."

"What time of day you want the wedding?" Gracie asked.

"In the early afternoon when it might be the warmest."

What about the bugs? There's bound to be hordes of lady bugs and slow crawling flies on everyone," griped Libby, visibly shuttering.

"We will lay paper fans on each of the chairs. Folks can swat the bugs," answered Molly, not about to let Libby damper her wedding plans.

"I'm thinking we should decorate the gazebo, shouldn't we?" asked Moxie, blinking her blue eyes excitedly.

"Yes, how about pink and white ribbons scalloped around the outside. Maybe some pink roses in the middle of each scallop. My bouquet will be pink roses along with baby's breath," planned Molly.

"Saints Preserve Us! Sounds beautiful to me. Sure and it tis, I'll be glad to do the decoratin'," agreed Moxie, clasping her hands together. She stared dreamily at the ceiling while she pictured the scene.

"Sounds to me like you've done some serious thinking on this subject already," teased Orie, looking lovingly at Molly.

"A girl has to be prepared with details for the wedding ceremony just in case she's asked, doesn't she?" Molly replied, winking at Orie. She continued on, "Uncle Malachi, you're in charge of getting the lawn chairs out of the carriage house and setting them in rows in front of the gazebo. You'll have to make sure the grass is cut, and the hedge is trimmed by then."

"Yes ma'am, but that's an awful lot of work for me to do all by myself in such a hurry," the elderly man moaned.

"I'll help you, Uncle Malachi. Between the two of us men we should be able to handle it," offered Orie

"Thank ya, sir," said Malachi, gratefully.

"You'll have a reception," said Melinda.

"I expect I should. I'll have a wedding cake baked. We can have some pink punch. That could be set up on a table behind the chairs for Sara to serve."

"I remember my wedding reception." Melinda voice trailed off. She relaxed back in her chair with a far away look on her face.

"What was it like?" Molly wanted to know.

"Tell us about it," encouraged Moxie.

"We had a dance in my father's barn until the wee hours of the morning. It was the most romantic thing I ever dreamed of. The smell of sweet, clover hay, the laughter of well wishers having a good time and fiddle music to dance to." Melinda sighed as she slapped her chest. Her brooch watch cover snapped open. The tune *Sentimental Journey* began. Melinda blushed and closed the cover. She looked over at Gracie. "I'm sorry."

"Haven't you got that dang latch fixed yet?" Gracie growled.

"No, I keep forgetting," Melinda said sheepishly.

Molly reached across and patted Melinda's knee. "Never mind Miss Gracie. The fun of having that watch is listening to the tune. We like to hear it."

Melinda lifted her chin defiantly at Gracie. Gracie straightened up in her chair, getting ready to defend herself. Before they two of them could start at each other, Molly kept going. "Miss Melinda, your wedding dance sounds like a lot of fun. After the wedding, we'll have the reception here. In the evening we could have a barn dance. Orie, can we use your

24

barn loft for the dance?"

"Oh I don't know," he groaned. "It's the wrong time a year for a barn dance."

"He's right," scoffed Gracie. "Why do you think people plan weddings in the spring and early June? So the loft won't be full of hay, that's why."

"Yes, I just put up the last crop of hay. The loft's full. I'd have to move it all out for a dance. Would you rather wait until next spring to get married when the loft's empty?" he asked, a twitch beginning at the corners of his mouth.

"I most certainly don't want to wait until spring. Could you clean the loft out please?" Molly pleaded.

"Oh yes, please, Mr. Orie. I'd like to go to one more barn dance before I'm too old to climb up the ladder to the loft," said Melinda, wistfully.

"All right," said Orie, reluctantly. "I'll hire the neighbor to help me toss the hay down in the barn, but everyone is mighty busy with corn picking right now. There's the lumber to buy and haul in to build the steps up to the loft. Plus, I just volunteered to help Uncle Malachi in the back yard. I hope I'm ready by the time you are for this wedding, Molly."

"Reckon ah could come hep you build the steps, sir," offered Malachi.

"That would be great. See Uncle Malachi helped to solve the problem. Thank you," said Molly, smiling at the older man.

"Onliest seems fair, Mr. Orie, ifen you's goen to hep me with the yard work."

"Neither one of you should worry. Whatever doesn't get done, we won't worry about. We're having this wedding on time. Deal?" declared Molly, patting Orie's hand.

"Deal!" said Orie, adamantly

"What about a bridal shower?" Moxie asked.

"No, I don't think that's necessary. It's not like we're just starting out. I expect there will be some wedding gifts, but there's no need for a shower," decided Molly. "Now how about we call it a night and start fresh tomorrow, ladies. You'll think better when you're fresh. You look like you're about to fall asleep on me."

Chapter 3

The very next morning after breakfast, Gracie and Melinda rocked in quiet rhythm, waiting for the workmen to arrive to install the telephone.

After a long silence, Melinda looked at Gracie. "Molly said we could invite someone to the wedding. Who you going to invite?"

"No one. I don't have any kin folk. My parents were older when I was born. I'm an only child. Now all my kin are dead. Why at my age, I know more folks in the cemeteries than I do living."

"Mercy, Gracie. What a thing to say," criticized Melinda, wrinkling up her nose.

Gracie shrugged her shoulders and softly patted her rocker arm. "Oh well, wouldn't of made much difference anyway. My folks wasn't much for going to weddings."

"I wish I had someone I could ask, but I don't have any relatives that I know of."

"What do you mean that you know of?"

"Perhaps there are offsprings of my brother's somewhere. I just don't know where. My sister, Lorena, died before she had a chance to marry. My husband died young before we started a family so as far as I know I'm alone, too. Why didn't you ever marry Gracie? You might not be alone now if you'd gotten married."

Gracie rubbed her hands together as if to warm them while she answered. "Just never did. Had a chance once, but I didn't take it. No need worrying about it now. Had to take care of my folks until I got too old for a man to look at. You never did say what took your husband."

"It was a horrible accident. I don't like to talk about it much even though it happened a long time ago. It still feels like yesterday to me when I think about it," said Melinda. Her voice quivered. She looked off into space as she caressed the mourning bracelet on her wrist with a finger. "That's why I wear this. It makes me feel like he's still with me somehow."

Opening the locket trimmed in black on the gold band, Melinda held her wrist over for Gracie to see the soft, curly whisks of brown hair. Melinda snapped the locket shut, let out a long, deep sigh and clasped her trembling hands together in her lap. The words spilled out of her. "It was in the spring. James was helping dig Elmer Hanson's grave, a well to do banker. Gave a good deal of what he earned back to this community. Do you remember him?"

"Reckon the name is familiar. My family never had anything to do with banks in them days. Pa always said it wasn't a safe thing to put all your eggs in one basket." Gracie paused to think about that then added. "Seems to me like a strange thing to say now that I think about it since he kept his money in an old sock under the straw mattress on his bed. Go on with what you was saying."

"Just when James and the two men helping him thought they had the grave dug, some of the soil caved back into the hole. My husband climbed down into the grave to clean it back out. The dirt had crumbled from under the banker's fancy monument. The men told me everything happened so fast. The monument toppled over and fell in on James, crushing him. One of those tall, white marble ones that weighs an awful lot. The other grave diggers tried digging down beside the grave to pull James out from under the stone, but by the time they got down to him it was too late. The three dollars James earned that day, I had to pay those other two men to dig my husband's grave." Melinda said mournfully. She pulled her hanky out of her skirt pocket and wiped a tear that slid down her face.

"That's awful. I'm right sorry to hear it," said Gracie, her voice huskier than usual. Rocking in sympathetic silence, Gracie patiently waited for Melinda to speak again.

"Anyway as for the rest of my family, my sister and brother moved away from here when they were old enough to leave home. I was the middle child. There was several years difference in our ages. Mother lost a baby between each of us. I did get word when my younger sister, Lorena, passed away. She died young. Don't know what from. She wasn't speaking to me when she left home so I'm surprised anyone bothered to let me know she died. By the time I heard of her passing it was too late to go to the funeral. Of course by that time, I wasn't sure she'd have wanted me there anyway." Her voice trailed off for a moment until she got her second wind. "My brother, Hiram Armstrong, moved away right after his wedding which was several years before I got married, him being older. I never heard from him again."

"What did your sister get mad about?" Gracie asked, trying to sound casual as she pried.

"I'd rather not say." Melinda answered quickly.

"Mind if I join you," interrupted Molly, opening the screen door. "It's a nice morning, but cool. Are you two sure you're warm enough.

We're fine Miss Molly. It's much nicer today. The cool spell is over for awhile, I hope," said Gracie.

"Well, enjoy it while you can. The temperature will get too cold soon for you to spend time outside," forecast ed

29

Molly.

Melinda cleared her throat and asked, "Have you decided where you're going on your honeymoon, Miss Molly?"

Molly's face glowed with excitement. "To New York City first.   We want to see some plays and eat in the fancy restaurants. Thought we'd take a train trip through some of the New England states to see the fall foliage. What do you think?"

"Sounds romantic to me," sighed Melinda. "Reminds me of my honeymoon. We went on a train trip down to Georgia. That was in early summer though."

"Orie will have his crops harvested by the wedding. Nothing pressing to do on the farm so we're going to take our time. We'll be gone a month, but back in time to have Thanksgiving with you. Do you think you'll be all right with me gone that long?" Worry lines wrinkled Molly's brow.

"We'll manage," grunted Gracie.

"Well, I'm putting Moxie in charge of things so if you have any problems you can have her help you with them."

"I don't know …," started Gracie.

Melinda interrupted Gracie by backhanding her on the shoulder. Gracie glared at her. Melinda gave her a hard look and spoke up. "That's fine. Miss Moxie will do a fine job of taking care of things, Miss Molly. You just go on that honeymoon and don't worry about anything."

It past through Gracie's mind that Moxie was one more reason that Nora Moser shouldn't have sent her daughter to boarding school out east all those years ago. That's where Molly met her friend Maxine McEntire. The nickname Moxie got tacked onto her because of her spunky ways. Short in stature and with curly, flaming red hair flowing from her head, Moxie always reminded Gracie of a wobbly newborn colt trying to keep up with the mare when she hurried after Molly.

Gracie didn't know if Moxie's problem was an eastern thing or not, but trying to keep up in a conversation with her was nearly impossible. She had an infuriating habit of going the long way around when she explained anything and with very distinctive, Irish accented words. Melinda always defended Moxie by saying she meant well, but Gracie thought the lady must have been born under an unlucky star. Seemed like everything she went to do went awry somehow for whoever she tried to help. *Just the kind of person to stay away from if you had a choice,* thought Gracie, but right now she felt outnumbered so she best keep her mouth shut.

"Just the same I will worry about all of you," Molly continued. "I've not been away from home for years. A month will seem like a long time. Having a telephone will help. I'll be able to call home while I'm gone."

"Where are you going to have the men put the telephone?" Gracie asked.

"I thought it could be put in the hallway so everyone can use it. I'm going to miss all of you so much I'd like to call home once in a while just to hear your voices."

"That's so sweet, Miss Molly, but remember you're suppose to be on your honeymoon so don't forget you have a husband," teased Melinda.

"Golly Moses, I won't forget that. Not for one moment," she said, laughing heartily.

"What Melinda's trying to say is stopped worrying about us. We made it this far in life on our own. Another month won't bother us. Just go and have fun," barked Gracie.

"Here comes the men with the telephone now," said Molly, pointing down the street. "Come on in, gentlemen. I'll show you where to put it."

One of the men carried a shiny, wooden, square box

with a receiver dangling by his side. The other man had a roll of wire. The men threaded the wire through a hole they drilled in the wall near the porch ceiling. They stretched the wire to the pole across the street in Sara's yard. Pulling the wire tight as they could, they secured it to that post. The wire still drooped down over the yard and street.

Gracie didn't like the look of that ugly wire swinging so low. She told the workers that. One of them assured her that they would put a pole up in the yard as soon as they could to secure the wire high in the air. That didn't make Gracie any happier. An ugly pole in the front yard might obscure her view of the neighborhood. If Molly had asked her opinion about the telephone, Gracie would have gladly told her it wouldn't have hurt her to wait a month to hear their voices until she got home. She wouldn't have to go to all this bother and expense, but reckon it was too late now to complain. Molly already had her heart set on this new contraption.

"Melinda, I'm going in after our quilts." Gracie rose and started to the door. "I meant to bring them out when I came, but I plain forgot to do it. Don't know where my mind goes these days."

Gracie walked down the hall past Miss Molly and the men. They didn't seem to notice her as they concentrated on getting the telephone box straight on the hall wall. Miss Molly was instructing the workers to secure the telephone low enough the elderly women could reach it without standing on tiptoes.

That morning, Gracie carried the lap quilts from upstairs down to the parlor as she went to breakfast, thinking that she wouldn't have to worry about making another trip up the stair steps. What did she do? Left them on the piano bench with the intentions of picking them up when Melinda and she went outside. She was in such a hurry to see what was going on over at the Bullock place, she plain forgot about the quilts.

Gracie walked out into the hall, shaking her head at how forgetful she had become. She stopped thinking about herself when she noticed Molly, standing by herself in the hall. Leaning against the wall with a forlorn look on her face, the young woman stared up at the row of Moser ancestral portraits across from her. Tears glistened in her eyes.

"Is there something wrong?" Gracie gathered the quilts under one arm and shifted them to her hip. She put her free hand on Molly's shoulder.

Molly turned to her and patted Gracie's hand. Swiping at a tear that rolled down her cheek, she pointed at one of the pictures. "That portrait there is my mother, Nora Moser. The one next to her is my father, Ned."

"Yeah, you showed them to us before," said Gracie. Nice enough looking couple with sour pickle expressions, wearing black clothes. Must have taken forever to snap their pictures from the look of their pop eyed stares. They didn't much like having their pictures taken from the looks of things. "Your ma was a nice looking woman. Her face is a might thinner than yours, but you look a lot like her."

"Do you think so? She was such a pretty person. Father was special, too. I was always his little girl. Guess they both spoiled me rotten."

"You'd never know it. Tell me what's got into you."

"I started to walk past the family portraits, and I couldn't help wishing my parents could be at my wedding."

Gracie searched for something comforting to say. She wished that Melinda was there. She always said the right thing. "Well, I reckon they will be. In spirit."

"I hope so. I've been wondering, Miss Gracie, do you think people would think me awfully odd if I put these portraits of my parents on chairs at the wedding to make me feel like they were there?"

"I've never been one who gave a horse's rear end what anyone else thought. I say if you want your folks pictures at your wedding then do it."

Molly giggled at Gracie's bluntness. "Oh thank you, Miss Gracie. I'm lucky. I know that. I'll have Aunt Pearlbee and Uncle Malachi to give me away. I have you, Miss Melinda and Miss Libby and Moxie to be at the wedding for me. I guess I shouldn't take on so."

"Nothing wrong with missing your ma and pa. No matter how old you get, you'll think about them at every special occasion in your life and wish they could be here. That's only natural. Just remember they'd be proud of you no matter what you did."

Molly studied her mother's picture. "I don't know. I'm not so sure my mother would want me to marry Orie." Wrinkle lines ran across her forehead.

"The past is long gone now. Miss Molly, you listen to me. First off, your ma would want you to be happy. Now that you're older and wiser if Mr. Orie is still the man that makes you happy, your ma would think your decision to marry him is just fine," Gracie assured her.

"You think so."

"I know so. Now I best get Melinda's quilt to her before she freezes to death."

"Thank you, Miss Gracie." Molly gave her a hug.

Settling down in her rocker, Gracie had just spread the quilt on her lap when she heard a succession of loud, tinny sounds echo down the entry hall. She slanted her head over her shoulder to listen. Molly's voice said, "Hello. Yes, I can hear you fine, Sara.

"Listen, Miss Molly's talking to Sara on the telephone," said Melinda. "I want to go talk to Sara. Let's go in."

Before Gracie had time to get out of her rocker, Melinda was through the door and down the hall. "Miss Molly can we talk to Sara on the telephone?"

"Of course, you can," said Molly, handing Melinda the receiver.

"Hello," yelled Melinda into the center of the telephone.

"My goodness," Molly said with a laugh. "Don't shout. You'll cause Sara to go deaf."

"Oh my, I'm sorry. Here, Gracie, you try it," said Melinda, shoving the receiver at Gracie.

"Sara, you there?" boomed Gracie. She listened for a second. "Reckon, that's right." She dropped the receiver back into the gold cradle on the side of the box.

"What did Sara say?" Molly asked, puzzled by Gracie hanging up so quickly.

"She said if we're going to yell at her, we might as well go out on the porch and do it. As close as she lives to us, we didn't need a telephone for that. I agreed with her."

Molly opened her mouth to speak, but before she could Gracie walked back out the screen door with a slight limp. She plopped down in her rocker, thrust her quilt up to her waist, and began to rock energetically. All the while, she glared at the Bullock telephone pole as though she'd like to put a curse on it. A fluffy cloud suspended behind the pole reminded her of a marshmallow skewered by a gigantic toothpick. How dare they deface her view of the only remnant of sky she could still see. How dare they do that in the name of progress.

35

Chapter 4

The next morning at breakfast, Molly said, "I've decided that I'd like to wear my mother's wedding gown. It's in the attic somewhere, but finding it will take a while. Would any of you like to help me look for it in that dusty mess?"

"Sounds like fun," agreed Melinda.

"I guess I can. I was just about to the end of a good book, but if this is the only way to get you a wedding dress, I'll go," grumped Libby. "But I'm not staying up there if I see spiders crawling around. I'll tell you that right now."

"I can't promise there won't be spiders, but thank you, Miss Libby, for wanting to help me," said Molly.

"I don't have anything better to do," consented Gracie, shrugging her shoulders.

"Perk up. Ye should think of it as a grand, treasure hunt, ladies. What fun to look through mementos in the attic for Molly's mother's lovely, wedding dress," exclaimed Moxie.

"Don't be too sure about it being fun. What's in that attic is more like junk then mementos," said Molly, giving a hearty laugh.

She led the way up the winding staircase and past her bedroom on the left and Moxie's on the right. At the end of the hall, the door on one side was to the water closet and on the other the stairs to the attic.

Holding a candle, Molly led the way up the narrow and steep steps. "Watch your steps, ladies. I don't want any of you falling down these stairs and breaking a leg right before my wedding," she cautioned.

At the stop of the stairs the light was so dingy, Gracie

paused out of the way to let her eyes adjust. She was afraid of running into or tripping over one of the stacks of suitcases, valises, wooden crates and steamer trunks all jumbled together, covered with dust and strung together with cobwebs. The women scattered out down the aisles between the stacks.

Inspecting a streamer trunk, Gracie deduced that might have been the one that the Mosers used on their long trips. All kinds of scratches and nicks let the wood show through the ivory paint. Narrow bands of tin held the well constructed trunk together. A heavy medal handle on each side curled around brackets. Just above the keyhole in trunk, Gracie stuck her fingers in a hollowed out spot. She struggled to raise the heavy lid with her arthritic hand.

Gracie picked up a pair of small, white, knitted booties and ran two of her fingers into the toe. "This trunk is full of baby things." She dropped the booties back into the trunk. "Reckon this must be your christening dress, Miss Molly." She held up a tiny, white, satin dress with a long, lace covered skirt. Three heart shaped, pearl buttons decorated the bodice. Gracie laid the dress back in trunk. She shook her head in wonder. "There looks to be enough baby clothes in this old trunk for at least two babies. Was all this yours, Miss Molly?"

"Yes, I expect so. I probably had anything I wanted and then some, and my mother never threw anything away."

"Just like my ma. It's a good thing she didn't. You'll be in need of those baby things some day," predicted Gracie.

"Let me get through the wedding first before I start a family, Miss Gracie." Molly blushed, giggling nervously.

Libby struggled with the clasp of a brown, tapestry valise. She dropped it. Out spilled dozens of old tin types. "What a mess. Nothing but picture, and I had to spill them."

"Members of my family that are long gone. Some day I

should take the time to put all those pictures in an album to keep for my children. I wouldn't mind looking at them myself. It's been so long since Mother showed them to me as a child. It's a pity to say, but I may not remember who some of those people are. Oh well, that'll be a good winter project."

Gracie was almost past a heap of books when she noticed an exposed piece of shiny wood in the middle of the pile. Quickly, she scooted the books off onto the floor into new piles and uncovered a sturdy, wooden rocker. Immediately, she sat down in it. Slowly, she rocked, shifting from one hip to the other to check out how comfortable the rocker felt.

"Look what I found. I used to have a rocker like this one. I left it with the other furniture in my house for the renters. I always wished I could have brought it here with me." Lovingly, she rubbed the wide, smooth arms."

"Looks like it's seen it's better days," grumped Libby.

"Miss Gracie, would you like this rocker taken to your room," offered Molly.

"Could I have it?" Gracie asked brightly.

"Of course, you can. Uncle Malachi can dust it off and take it down to your room."

Gracie gave the young woman a warm look. "Much oblige, Miss Molly. I'll like having this old rocker to sit in when look out the window this winter."

"Your room's a good place to hide that old rocker if you ask me. Aren't we suppose to be looking for a wedding gown? Let's find it and get out of this dirty place before Gracie wants to take all this junk downstairs," grumped Libby.

"To be sure, you're right. Keep lookin' everyone. The clock is ticking a countdown to Molly's weddin' day. We don't have a minute to waste," Moxie agreed with Libby.

While the others stood around the rocker Gracie found,

Melinda wandered back to one corner of the attic to a stack of wooden crates piled higher than her head. Standing on tiptoes, she reach up, put her hands on the ends of the crate at the top and tried to scoot it over the edge. Finding it heavier than she expected, she tugged hard to drag the crate toward her. The whole stack of crates teetered. Giving a yelp, she let go of the crate and backed out of the way just as the crates toppled. When the cloud of dust cleared away, a heap of thin, wood fragments from the broken crates, dried out from years of storage, lay at Melinda's feet.

When Melinda cried out, the other ladies watched the crates fall. "Are you all right, Miss Melinda?" Molly scrambled around a row of steamer trunks to get to the elderly woman.

"Yes, I'm fine," she cried between sniffles and sneezing. As she looked at the mess in front of her, her eyes widened. She exclaimed, "I think I found the wedding dress." Gently, she pulled on a portion of bodice sticking out of a smashed carton at her feet.

"What a mess," grumped Libby. "I hope you don't expect me to help you clean up all this --." she stumbled, trying to find a better word then continued, "mess. Melinda, you should be more careful."

"I do hope the gown is all right after taking such a tumble. I'm so sorry Miss Molly," apologized Melinda, wiggling a finger at the broken crates.

"Don't worry about it, dear. The attic needs cleaning up. This will give Uncle Malachi something to do this winter when he can't work outside." Molly took the dress from Melinda. She shook it, then held it up while Gracie and Moxie removed the pieces of broken crate from the skirt. She shook it again and held it against herself. A lace over skirt trimmed with a row of white lace around the bottom covered the long, full satin skirt fastened to a tight bodice. The first row of lace on the bodice came to a v at the waist. The top row covered the whole top of the bodice and laid just over the bottom row of lace. The neckline had a high lace collar that curled out at the top. Slim sleeves had a wide piece of lace dropping down from the shoulders and ended with four inch cuffs trimmed in lace.

"Looks like Mother was some bigger than I am in the middle. This gown is going to need altering," Molly decided.

"I used to be a good seamstress. Could I do that for you?" asked Melinda, enthusiastically.

"That would be very nice. Thank you."

"I thought you told me your fingers were too stiff to sew anymore," Gracie said.

"I can still do some sewing. Just not for long periods of time like when I altered for a living. Working on Miss Molly's wedding gown will be fun," Melinda assured them all.

That afternoon Molly, Moxie and Gracie walked downtown. While Molly stopped in the Locked Rock Review to order the wedding invitations, Gracie and Moxie went to the post office. Near the front door, the postmistress, Cherry Bright, swiped her corn straw broom back and forth across the rough, board floor, gathering up the oily, sawdust sweep she had scattered to clean the floor. Gracie made a wide birth around the floor sweep to keep from getting any on the soles of her shoes. Moxie followed her lead.

"Hello," greeted Mrs. Bright. "Came for the Moser mansion mail, I expect." It being more of a statement than a question, she didn't wait for a reply. She stopped sweeping and walked behind the counter. She turned to face the rows of small, wooden cubicles fastened to the wall. Reaching into a cubicle that was stuffed full, she turned and gave the handful of mail to Moxie.

Later in the parlor, everyone sat patiently waiting while Moxie played postman. Shuffling through the envelopes, she sorted out a hand full. "Molly, sure and these are for ye." Going back through the remaining letters, Moxie read out loud, "Melinda Applegate. Whoa!" Moxie took a second look.

"I got a letter?" Melinda asked, clapping her hands.

"That's what it says, but there's no return address on it," said Moxie, mystified.

"Are you sure, Miss Moxie? Melinda never gets any mail," said Gracie.

Moxie took another look. "Yes, that's what it says. It's for ye, Miss Melinda."

"Who'd be writing to me?" Melinda puzzled as she tore open the envelope and unfolded the letter.

Gracie leaned forward, watching her face for a reaction. She relaxed when she saw Melinda smile. "What does the letter say? Who's it from?"

"Now, Miss Gracie," scolded Molly. "Miss Melinda's letter is private. We shouldn't pry into her business." Clearly, a curious look was pasted on Molly's face, too.

"That's all right, Miss Molly. I want to tell you. It's from a nephew. His name is Jeffrey Armstrong."

"You said you didn't know your relatives," Gracie said.

"I didn't, and I still don't. I didn't want to say anything in case nothing came of it, but I decided to send a letter to the Reader to Reader column in the Topeka Daily Capital, asking for contact with my brother, Hiram. or any descendants of his. Apparently his son saw the letter and decided to answer it. Isn't that wonderful?" Hugging the letter to her chest, Melinda was so happy about hearing from her nephew, she didn't notice the concerned looks on the other women's faces.

Chapter 5

The next few weeks came and went much too fast. Apprehension hung over Moser Mansion. It seemed as though all the wedding preparations would never get done by the day of the event. After he finished picking his corn, Orie showed up to help Malachi with the yard work. When Gracie asked how Orie was coming with arrangements for the barn dance, he grumbled that he still had to haul home the lumber from the saw mill to make the steps to the barn loft. That would all take time but hopefully soon Malachi and he would have the yard work done, and they could tackle building the steps.

A burst of Indian summer kept everyone hopeful that the temperature the day of the wedding would be comfortably warm. Melinda, cloistered away in her bedroom, worked on altering Molly's wedding gown. With Orie coming over so often, she wanted to make sure he didn't accidentally see the gown before the wedding day.

Libby Hook stayed quietly out of the way in the library. She likely assumed there would be less likelihood that anyone would ask her to help if she was out of sight. That was one woman that Gracie didn't think she could ever hit it off with. A tall, thin lady, she always seemed peculiar. To keep peace in the mansion, Gracie tried to avoid Libby as much as possible.

Left to her own company, Gracie sat in the gazebo so she could watch the men work. Malachi push the reel mower passed her, up and down the shaggy lawn. She tried to keep her mind on what the handyman was doing to shake the feeling of being lonely enough to put up with even Libby. No matter how hard she tried her mind strayed to Libby when she looked at the empty wicker chair beside her. Gracie chided herself for having thoughts of inviting Snippy Libby to join her and for missing Melinda's company. She'd been alone for the better part of her life. She had been used to that before she came to the Moser mansion. In fact, Gracie thought she had resigned herself to always being alone. When she let herself think about what it had been like living on her farm and the difference now that she lived with the other women at the mansion, she decided she must have gone soft in her old age. When Gracie thought back to when she was young, she had truly loved life on the farm by herself. Now she just had too much time on her hands was all. Time to think about things she didn't want to think about like being alone, families and love. After all the wedding would be over in a matter of weeks. She just had to be patient. Things would go back to normal.

Orie showed up early that morning. He backed his team along the backside the hedge. Energetically, he tackled the hedge trimming with a pair of clippers and piled one armload of the brush after another in his wagon to haul back to the farm to burn.

Gracie straightened in her chair. Suddenly, it dawned on her while she watched the handsome, young man work, things may never be as she knew them in Moser Mansion again. After the honeymoon, a man would live in the house. That would take some getting used to. Gracie hadn't lived in the same house with a man since her father passed away in their farm house years before. She wondered if Melinda had given any thought to Orie coming to live with them. When Melinda came out of hiding, Gracie would ask her what she thought about that. Would they be able to walk to the water closet in their nightgown? Would they be able to talk about whatever they wanted to in front of Orie? Would he leave messes everywhere? Orie being a farmer, he'd be bound to track up the floors when he came home. Would Molly be able to get him to clean up and change clothes before he sat down to eat a meal on her fancy furniture? Gracie grinned at the thought of Molly confronted with that dilemma. If Molly had rough hewn furniture like the sturdy table and chairs that Gracie's father built for her farm house, she wouldn't have to worry.

What about Libby? Gracie cackled out loud as she imagined Libby wrinkling up her nose at the hog odor on Orie's clothes. She could imagine Libby heading off to a far corner with a hanky over her nose. What else would happen that Gracie couldn't imagine after so many years of not having a man around? *Best quit worrying about what will be until it gets here. Molly's happy. That's all that matters.*

Looking at the tall, alabaster, angel bird bath that doubled as a bird feeder in the winter, Gracie couldn't help grinning as her thoughts turned back to August when Mavis Jordan threatened Melinda and her. Mavis tried to get away from Orie and ran smack dab into that angel. She fell to her knees and stayed there just long enough for Gracie to push her down to the ground. Gracie and Melinda plopped down on that she killer's backside until Sheriff Ben Logan arrested her for murdering Rachel Simpson. That was the only excitement the backyard had seen through the years until the coming wedding. Orie and Molly's wedding was a different kind of safe excitement that Gracie had no part in except to watch take place, but it would do. *Being bored was no fun,* she vowed even if she had to get gussied up.

"Gracie, come on in," Melinda shouted out the back door, waving her hand excitedly. "I have the alterations done on the wedding gown. Miss Molly's going to try it on for us."

44

"All right, I'll be right there," answered Gracie, slowly lifting herself from the wicker chair.

"Can I come too?" Orie called from behind the hedge.

"Certainly not! It's bad luck for the groom to see the bride in her gown before the wedding," Melinda protested with her hands on her hips.

"You keep working, Mr. Orie. You're behind as it is," ordered Gracie.

"Yes, ma'am," Orie replied contritely, stepping through the hedge. He tipped his hat at her. Gracie noted a twitch at the corners of his mouth.

Molly, eager to try the gown on, took it to her bedroom while Gracie, Melinda and Libby sat on Melinda's bed, waiting for her to come back. In a few minutes, Molly appeared. She had the outstretched gown in her arms. Her face was full of disappointment.

"Why haven't you got the gown on?" Melinda asked hesitantly.

"Well, there seems to be a problem," said Molly.

"What is it?" Melinda went to meet her, concern written all over her face.

"Oh Miss Melinda, the waist of the gown is too small now. I tried to slip it over my head, but couldn't get it past my underarms. What are we going to do?" Molly held the dress up to her, looking distraught.

Melinda gave her a hug. Smiling reassuringly, she spoke in her calm, soft voice, "I'm sorry. I must have taken the side seams up too much but that's not a problem. Really it isn't so don't worry, dear. I didn't cut away any of the material in the seams. All I have to do is let the seams out and start over."

Molly's face flooded with relief then with anxiety again. Gracie looked from Molly to Melinda. Molly had to be

45

wondering if she gave Melinda another chance, would she be successful, or if she should take the gown downtown to the dress shop seamstress. Time was running out. Molly needed to know the gown would fit. Wrestling with her decision, she looked down at the gown in her hands and back at Melinda's imploring face. The elderly woman was so anxious to be helpful. Molly couldn't hurt her feelings. She decided to give Melinda another chance.

In a few days, Melinda announced that the alterations were done again and invited everyone to her room to wait for Molly to try it on. Molly left the bedroom with the wedding gown over her arms, holding it high to keep it from dragging on the floor.

The wait seemed endless as the older ladies watched the door for Molly's return. She was gone longer than the first time. Libby pushed at wrinkles in the Dresden plate quilt around her. Gracie stared out the window at Orie and Malachi putting the finishing touches to the hedge, throwing the last of the limbs into the heaped wagon. Moxie sat quietly on the bed, staring at the doorway. Melinda paced the floor with fingers crossed on both hands, mumbling prayers.

Molly burst into the room and exclaimed, "Perfect!" She held the gown's full skirt out away from her on both sides. She swished first to one side then the other, modeling in front of the full length mirror behind Melinda's bedroom door.

Melinda walked around Molly, inspecting her sewing job with tears of relief in her eyes.

"I love the way Mother's wedding gown looks on me," said Molly to Melinda "and I love you for altering it for me." She gave Melinda a hug. "Mother would be so pleased that I'm getting married in her wedding gown. It makes me feel like she's part of my wedding. Well, how do I look, ladies?" Molly turned toward Moxie and Libby.

"You're absolutely lovely for sure and perfect for a wedding in that gown, me thinks," teased Moxie.

"I must say that gown is almost as pretty as the one I wore when I got married," was Libby's offhanded compliment.

"What about you, Miss Gracie? What do you think?" Molly asked.

"I think it will be just fine," offered Gracie, glancing briefly at Molly before she turned back to the window. She wasn't quite sure how she should feel about a fancy dress like that and getting married. After all, she had never been in that situation before herself. No experience there. One thing was for sure, now she'd have Melinda back, keeping her company again. She'd be glad for that.

Chapter 6

A few days later, Moxie asked Gracie to walk downtown with her. Figuring the walk would do her good, Gracie consented to go along. Her shawl felt good, but the morning sun had started to warm up the chill in the air. By the time they headed for home, she hoped the sun succeeded. They were headed to the post office. and the Locked Rock Review newspaper to pick up the wedding invitations for Molly. The errands shouldn't take too long.

Main Street was quiet yet. Most people in the country still had harvesting to complete. The women hadn't seen Orie since he finished helping Malachi with the yard work. He said he had plenty to do on the farm. He needed to keep at it if he was to be done in time to leave on the honeymoon.

Gracie hugged her shawl tighter around her and hoped that the day of the wedding would be a bit warmer. *Reckon I'll have to ask Melinda to put in a word for good weather in one of those prayers of hers and see if that'll help,* she thought with a grin.

Later, Moxie and Gracie met the other residents of Moser Mansion in the parlor. Moxie handed Molly two small boxes of wedding invitations. Eagerly, she opened one of the boxes, and examined the top card. "They look fine. Want to see?" Molly handed the card to Moxie. She read it and passed it on to Gracie.

The invitation, a pearly, white card, had a row of tiny, pink roses across the top and bottom. In the middle, the card read, "Orie Lang and Molly Moser request your presence at their wedding on October 20, 1903 at one o'clock in the afternoon at the Moser Mansion in Locked Rock, Iowa. The garden wedding will be in the gazebo in the backyard with cake and punch after the nuptials. That evening you are invited to the Orie Lang farm for a barn dance in honor of the couple."

As soon as they had all inspected the wedding invitation, Moxie thumbed through the pile of letters in her hand and began mail call. "Libby Hook. Looks like it's from your son in California."

"Oh good. I invited him and his wife to come to the wedding. I hope that's all right, Miss Molly." She looked uncertainly at Molly..

"Of course, it is. I told all of you to invite someone. Now we have the official invitations to send your son," assured Molly.

Libby tore open the envelope and read the letter. A sad look crossed her face. When she finally spoke, her voice held a flat note. "No need to send my son an invitation. He says he's much too busy to come so far for a wedding."

That didn't surprise Gracie. A long time ago, she suspected the fact was sad but true that Libby's son probably preferred to live as far away from his mother as he could and was happy to keep it that way. Gracie put her attention on Moxie when she spoke, "Molly, sure and here tis several letters for you."

"Probably from some of my out of town relatives. I wrote to them that I was engaged and not to be surprised if they received a wedding invitation soon."

"Melinda Evans," Moxie recited. She took a quick, second look. "Whoa! No, I was right. The envelope's addressed to Miss Melinda."

"For me!" Melinda cried, holding her hand out.

"That's what it says," answered Moxie, depositing the envelope in the elderly woman's trembling hand.

"Who'd be writing to me this time?" Melinda stared at the envelope.

"Open it and find out," ordered Gracie, impatiently.

"Looks to be from that nephew that wrote to ye awhile back from the looks of the handwriting," offered Moxie, standing beside her to peer down at the envelope. "Wonder why the gentleman never puts a return address on his letters."

Melinda looked at the envelope, shrugged her shoulders and quickly tore it open. She pulled out a sheet of paper and scanned it.

"Well, what does it say?" asked Gracie.

"Now, Miss Gracie, don't pressure Miss Melinda. Let her read the letter in peace," scolded Molly, leaning forward herself.

"It's from my nephew. Jeffrey says he'd love to come to escort me to your wedding. Oh, I hope it's all right. I've already invited him," cried Melinda gleefully. "Isn't that wonderful? I have found a relative, and he's coming to see me."

Chapter 7

Finally, the big day was almost upon them. Everyone in the mansion retired early the night before the wedding, worn out from the excitement and anticipation.

The old house's creaks and groaned while Gracie tossed and turned. Too keyed up to sleep, she decided to get up and try out the rocker Malachi placed in front of the window. She sat down, covered with a glowing square provided by the large, orange, harvest moon. Tapping the tip of her toes on the floor, she rocked. All sort of thoughts tumbled through Gracie's mind. Tomorrow was a big day for Molly. The life of Molly and everyone in the mansion would change with Orie living there.

Gracie hadn't lived in the same house with a man since her father died. If she hadn't taken care of him for so long and farmed the family land all those years by herself life would have been different for her. She leaned back in her rocker and closed her eyes, picturing the way it could have been.

Just before Pa got sick, she sparked with Millard Sokol. He seemed to be taken with her. It looked like he might be going to propose to her. She'd daydreamed about what she'd say if that happened. But Pa got sick. Gracie turned down Millard's requests to go out with him after that. Finally, he quit showing up to ask. At first Gracie was troubled by that and lonesome. She enjoyed a man's attention more than she wanted to admit and the fun of being at the dances with other young people. After awhile, she convinced herself that it was just as well Millard quit coming. Gracie conjured up a picture in her mind of what he looked like, a short runt of a man no taller than her and plain looking. If she was to be honest with herself, what she liked best about him was his nice looking pair of horses and that nice buggy he always took her places in.

Gracie wondered why she should be thinking about Millard. That was water long gone under the bridge. A long time ago, she resigned herself to the fact that she'd never have a wedding. She'd never have a child or any other relative to do things with her. *Oh well, such is life. Best get in that bed and be rested up for the long day tomorrow.* She gave one last appreciative look at the moon, big, round and orange like a pumpkin without the jack o lantern face carved in it.

She changed her course on the way to bed. She headed out of her room to visit the water closet. In the dark, the hall seemed longer. It was a good thing she wasn't in a hurry to get to the water closet. As slow as she walked these days if she had an urgency to get there, she might not make it in time. Gracie crossed the hall, ran her hand along the wall over Moxie's closed bedroom door. Finally, she reached the water closet.

A dog let out a series of yips from behind the back yard hedge. Listening to the high pitched barks, Gracie couldn't resist pausing even though she now felt the need to hurry. She glanced out the window and determined the yapping was Maudie Brown's noisy beagle. A rabbit probably ran in front of the tied up dog, teasing him.

Readied for the wedding in front of the gazebo, moonlight bathed the rows of white chairs with a ghostly glow in the hushed stillness. An ominous dread that something was going to go wrong settled over Gracie. She always hated getting a premonition that something bad was going to happen. She turned the glass knob on the water closet door. The feeling would have to wait. She hoped it came from being tired and would disappear by morning.

Chapter 8

First thing the morning of the wedding, Gracie stuck her head out the front door and breathed a sigh of relief. She marched up to the kitchen table and announced, "We're in luck. Indian summer decided to hang around one more day to bless Molly's wedding."

Moxie praised, "Thank ye, Lord, the shining sun and its warmth. However, me thinks the Lord had a little help from the Moser family good luck omen."

"That good luck omen is rubbish," Gracie declared. "This beautiful day, calm and warm, can be contributed to Melinda's lengthy prayers before she went to sleep every night for the last week."

"In that case, thank you so much for your thoughtful prayers, Miss Melinda," said Molly.

"In deed, a fine help ye was," added Moxie.

Melinda blushed at the attention.

No one felt like eating Pearlbee's eggs, bacon and large golden biscuits in spite of the cook grumbling about listen to empty stomachs growl all morning. The ladies settled for coffee.

Molly started to ask Pearlbee to refill her cup. "No, I've changed my mind, Aunt Pearlbee.   I have the jitters bad enough without making it worse."

Pearlbee smiled, giving Molly a motherly look. She replied in her sage way, "Just keep tellin' yerself Miss Molly, yous gonna make it through this day and be glad yous did it."

She paused then said sagely, "Of course, yous gonna be glad when it's over, too."

"Golly Moses, did you hit that nail on the head, Aunt Pearlbee. I just have to keep telling myself to stay calm," said Molly, taking a deep breath.

Pearlbee fixed an early light lunch of ham sandwiches and firmly insisted that everyone eat at least one. After lunch, Libby went to her room to dress for the wedding, before she hid out in the peace and quiet of the library. Moxie and Sara left the house to decorate the gazebo with the supply of recently delivered pink roses. Gracie and Melinda adjourned to the porch to sit for the first time in a very long time. The moment was a taste of Gracie's familiar routine returning to what it had been before the mansion turned upside down because of Molly's wedding.

However, it didn't take long for Gracie to decide sitting with Melinda wasn't much fun. She fretted because she hadn't heard from her nephew about when he'd arrive. She worried that he'd be too late for the wedding. In fact, Melinda was a basket case. To get her mind off her nephew, Gracie suggested that they slip along the side of the house to see how decorating the gazebo was going.

Moxie and Sara had the pink and white ribbons twisted together and fastened in scallops at the bottom of the screens just like Molly wanted. They were in the process of wading back between the large, rose bushes to tack large, pink bows at the point of each ribbon scallop.

Gracie tried to eavesdrop on the two women, but they whispered. Gracie's hearing wasn't that good anymore. The uneasy feeling from the night before crept back over Gracie. Those two women sharing a secret might not be a good thing. Gracie thought about it a minute and decided to leave well enough alone. She nudged Melinda and nodded toward the porch. Best she didn't know what those two were hatching up.

Once settled in a rocker, Melinda leaned her head back. She closed her eyes and tried to relax, leaving Gracie to her own thoughts once again. She wondered how the two of them, such complete opposites, could get along as well as they did. A gentle lady, Melinda dressed in white, silky, ruffled blouses and bright colored skirts while Gracie preferred cotton blouses and full skirts in tans and browns. A special event such as a wedding was no exception to dress up. She wore the same tan blouse and brown skirt that she used for church on Sundays. She figured it saved on time trying to decide what to wear if she stuck to one good outfit. However, she had to admit that next to her getup, Melinda looked mighty fancy in her bright blue blouse with a large crocheted white, high necked, lace collar that draped over her shoulders. For contrast with the white blouse, she had on a black, form fitting velvet skirt. Pinned to the back of Melinda's hair was a large, white bow trimmed with blue to match her blouse.

A mop of natural curls, Melinda's light gray hair was the complete opposite of Gracie's dark gray braids that wound around her head, thinner now then they used to be. At least neither one of them had to make a fuss over their hair all the time to keep it looking nice. That was the only thing Gracie figured that they had in common.

Even the quilts on their laps were the exact opposite. The double wedding ring quilt on Melinda's lap, she had made from small, brightly colored scraps sewn together by hand to form rings that overlapped. Before her fingers became too stiff to sew, Melinda used tiny, even quilting stitches to fasten the back to the colorful front which took hours to do.

On the other hand, Gracie filled her quilt top with six

inch blocks of dark squares cut from old clothes; brown, tan and blacks sewn in rows. Gracie tacked the back to the top with twine knots from string she saved when she opened feed sack tops. Wasn't much to look at, but that quilt kept her just as warm as Melinda's was.

Melinda, lady like with a quiet soft voice, was a timid soul while brash sounding Gracie always got bluntly to the point. She'd been raised on a farm and dealt more with men than she did women. She hadn't seen the need to pick up the finer points of etiquette which seemed to come naturally to the other ladies of Moser Mansion. However, Melinda wasn't the only one that had a reason to be nervous. An occasion like this fancy wedding was enough to make Gracie uneasy, too. After all, this would be a vastly different day from their quiet every day routine of sitting on the porch watching the neighbors.

Glancing toward Main Street, Gracie spotted the tall, thin stranger dressed in a black suit, white shirt and bow tie, walking along the picket fence. Looked to be in his early thirties. Tuffs of black hair stuck out under his black, bowler hat. Everything about him spelled city slicker. A sure sign that he had to be related to Melinda. Either way anyone that dressed up, Gracie was pretty sure would be coming to the wedding if they wandered into toward the mansion.

Suddenly, the man stopped and turned quickly around. He flattened himself against the picket fence and looked behind him. A harried look past over his face when he turned back to survey the rest of the neighborhood past the Moser Mansion. Gracie straightened in her rocker. She narrowed her eyes, inspecting the stranger. She felt a curious uneasiness about his wary watchfulness. He acted as though he thought someone might be following him that he didn't want to meet. Of course, it might be only natural that he'd want to check out the area to see where his aunt lived. After all, he'd never been there before. Could be the man was worried that he might be lost?

"Melinda, here comes a stranger. Might be your nephew."

"You think so? Oh my, look how handsome he is," she gasped. She watched the young man walk along the fence.

The city slicker paused long enough to read the rest home sign and come through the gate. He looked up at the porch and spotted the ladies watching him. A nervous smile spread across his lips. He tipped his hat brim as he nodded at the two of them. Then he stood for an instant, checking the house over from one end to the other. Before he spoke, the young man whipped off his bowler hat and placed it over his chest. "Good afternoon, ladies. Would this be the Moser Mansion?"

"Might be. Who's asking?" Gracie replied curtly. It occurred to her that he might be a pesky Watkins salesman.

"My name is Jeffrey Armstrong. I am looking for my aunt, Melinda Applegate." His smile seemed pasted around his lips, never reaching his piercing, blue eyes. Cold eyes that might make folks feel like blocks of ice before he was done staring a hole through them. He'd clasped his hands together tightly as he spoke,. His fingers turned white.

"That's me," cried Melinda. She stood up and motioned for him to come onto the porch. Throwing her arms around his middle, she said, "I'm so proud to have you come see me."

"I'm not too late for the wedding am I, Aunt Melinda?"

"No, but I was getting nervous that you weren't going to make it in time."

"Coming by train, I just wasn't sure how long it'd take me. I worried I should have started sooner. Who is this lovely lady?" He turned to Gracie and bowed in an easy charming way. Gracie still wasn't sure about his smile. It seemed to have turned to a smirk with his inquiry about her when he turned away from his aunt. Besides his smooth talking words weren't the kind of compliment that Gracie was easy about taking to right off. With a growing uneasiness, she decided she'd rather he had been a salesman so they could send him on his way.

"My friend, Gracie Evans. She lives here in the ... at the mansion, too," Melinda finished.

"Nice to meet you, ma'am." The man held out his hand.

Gracie barely touched his fingers in a slight shake then quickly withdrew her hand. "Where did you come from on the train?" Gracie asked, looking the dude closely.

A slight lift of one of his eyebrows at her inspection showed his uncomfortableness. "Why from home," Jeffrey answered. Quickly, he turned his back on Gracie and spoke to his aunt. Too quickly to Gracie's way of thinking. "How soon do we have to start for the wedding, Aunt Melinda?"

"It's going to take place in the back yard. I'm afraid Miss Molly is already getting dressed so you'll have to wait until after the wedding to meet the bride and groom. Shall we go around back and get a seat up front?"

Nodding, Jeffrey stepped between the two ladies and offered both of them an arm. Melinda stuck her arm through the young man's, looking up at him proudly. Gracie, not knowing how to turn him down without hurting Melinda's feelings, accepted the arm he offered her, but she barely touched it with her fingertips as they walked.

Uneasy as she felt, she silently chided herself for being so suspicious of this stranger. She just met the young man. This was no time to form opinions of him that might be wrong. The last thing she wanted to do was hurt Melinda's feelings now that she was so happy at finding kin folk.

When the trio came in sight of the back yard, Jeffrey stopped abruptly. Gracie looked up at his face. He seemed to be studying the few, early guests with a pensive look. Was he expecting someone to be at the wedding that he didn't want to run into?

Melinda tugged on the young man's sleeve to get him started again, "Oh come on, Jeffrey. Sara already saved places for us. She'll show us where to sit. That's her over there at the end of those empty chairs."

Chapter 9

The romantic scent of roses filled the air. The three of them walked down the bridal path past the piano. Squirming around on the bench, Libby, with a curious look on her face, inspected Melinda's nephew. The woman looked quite nice for this special occasion. Her dark green dress had a pale green, turtle neck collar that covered up her long, skinny neck. The hat atop Libby's head matched the color of the dress. As was the style of the times, she'd slanted the hat to one side so that its small white crown was visible. The crown, surrounded by dark green, velvet trim crossed in back, hung down past the brim.

Watching Libby fidget, Gracie imagined that she could hardly wait to get her part of the wedding over with. Libby had a way of making anything she did for someone seem as if it was an obligation to her.

Sara Bullock came toward them in a pink dress with a white lace trimmed neckline. A hat of white, satin swirls complemented the new, curly hairdo she'd gotten just for the wedding. *More power to her,* thought Gracie. She couldn't imagine spending hours with her hair wrapped up in hot irons for any reason.

Sara led them to their seats. What struck Gracie's attention, she refrained from commenting on. A ridiculous string of large, pink roses entwined in green vines wound around Sara's shoulders like a Hawaiian lei. That had to be an eye catcher for everyone. Gracie imagined it'd also be a conversation piece for later, too.

Sara pointed out their seats. Jeffrey walked in three

seats and waited to sat down, Melinda sat next to him and Gracie on the outside before he took his seat. Sara started to make conversation. She was dying to pump Jeffrey for information about himself, but guests arrived. Sara stayed busy running back and forth across the yard, greeting and pointing out places to sit.

Amazing to Gracie was the amount of notables that showed up. A series of loud popping noises came from the direction of the street in front of the mansion. Gracie vowed she'd know that racket anywhere. The pops announced Phillip Harris's red, Vermont touring automobile as he slowed to a stop. She didn't believe anyone at the wedding dressed fancier than the Harris couple. Him in a fifty dollar suit and his wife, looking like a model for "The Delineator" fashion magazine, dressed in a slim, black skirt and jacket with gray brocaded flowers and swirls. Mrs. Harris's blouse had gray v shape trims and a gold flower pin at the base of the high neck. Her dark, red hat, a layer of red material holding a pile of small, red roses, sat directly atop her head, covering all her coal black hair except the wisps that lay over her ears and at the base of her neck.

Locked Rock mayor, James Long and his wife arrived next. Allegra Long looked dowdy in anything she wore. Too much of the middle age spread happening, but she did look as good as she could in a blue dress with a high buttoned collar. Her shawl was a white, squiggle affair that Gracie couldn't quite figure out, but her hat had to win the prize for being the most unusual. Two layers of blue velvet with white feathers oozing out between the layers to tickle Mrs. Long's ears. Another layer of feathers fluffed on top the hat.

Once again, Gracie studied her plain, cotton blouse and skirt. Just for a moment but only for a moment, she wished she'd come dressed in one of the high necked getups with the fancy hats. It came to her that the reason she was sitting in that uncomfortable lawn chair wasn't to look like something she wasn't. It was to see Molly and Orie hitched and starting a new, happy life together. How she looked right now, or anyone else here looked didn't matter compared to that. Besides Molly didn't mind how Gracie dressed as long as she was comfortable. She'd said so often enough. That meant a lot more to Gracie than what other folks thought of her plain getup.

As the chairs filled up around the second row, Gracie worried that someone tall would sit down in front of them and block her view of the wedding. She glanced down through the holes in the two chair backs in front of her. Each had something dark on the seat. She leaned forward to peer over the top of one of the chairs. It was the portrait of Molly's mother, Nora. On the other chair leaned the framed picture of Ned Moser.

Libby opened the watch pinned to her dress, and checked the time. She turned on the piano seat and began to play soft music. The guests quieted down to loud whispers and giggles, watching and waiting. The bride didn't appear. In a few minutes, people leaned toward each other and began a higher pitched buzz.

Gracie elbowed Melinda in the ribs. "I think we better go see what's keeping Miss Molly. Look at Mr. Orie and Earl in the gazebo, dancing on one foot then the other in front of the preacher. I don't know how long the bridegroom is going to be able to stand the suspense of waiting before he explodes. We better go see if the bride got cold feet and ain't coming."

"That's a ridiculous thing to say," Melinda said, giggling. "But we might be able to help speed her up. We'll be right back, Jeffrey. Save our seats for us."

"Will do," her nephew assured her.

Gracie and Melinda reached the open staircase just as Molly descended slowly with the skirt of her wedding gown gathered in her hands. Moxie followed behind, trying to hold the skirt up to keep it from dragging on the steps.

"Everyone's waiting. Are you about ready to get hitched or not?" demanded Gracie.

"I don't know. I mean yes. Oh, I reckon so," stammered Molly. She was flustered and rosy cheeked by the time she made it off the last step.

"You look lovely, dear." Melinda gave the bride a hug, knocking Molly's white, straw hat sideways on her head. Molly grabbed the heavy hat, covered with pink and white roses and a pink bow in back.

"I'm sorry about that, Miss Molly." Melinda reached up and leveled the hat. "Everything is going to be all right. Being nervous is natural," soothed Melinda.

"Reckon you better get out that door and get this wedding over with before you get cold feet," said Gracie, "or before the guests leave. They're getting mighty restless."

"Now stop that, Gracie" Melinda scolded. "Miss Molly's ready. Let's go back to our seats so we can see these pretty ladies walk out to meet Mr. Orie and Earl."

"Hurry up then," growled Gracie, marching to the door.

With a watchful eye on the back door, Orie looked ever bit as nervous as a bridegroom should. He tugged at the knot in his long, black tie. Clearly, the bridegroom uncomfortable in his black suit. Sure didn't look like the farmer, in overalls and straw hat, delivering milk, eggs and fresh vegetables to his customers.

Gracie stopped to whisper in Libby's ear that Molly was on her way. Libby changed to playing the wedding march. Gracie waited for Melinda to go past her then sat down. She watched the back door. No Molly, but an increase in buzzing from the guests.

Making a grand entrance in her pink gown, Moxie walked around the side of the house. A black, velvet ribbon ran through the high necked, lace collar and tied in a bow in back of her figure fitting dress. The brim on her hat, a narrow, oval shaped, braided flat piece, curved down in front and back. The middle of it was layers of black, velvet ribbon from which hung white cherries. On the under side the brim above each of her ears peeked a white crocheted rose.

"Who's the pretty bridesmaid, Aunt Melinda?" whispered Jeffrey.

"Miss Molly's friend, Moxie McEntire, from Boston. She lives with us now," shared Melinda.

Gracie feared that Moxie goofed again, making her entrance from the wrong place, but Molly appeared. She marched right behind her bridesmaid between Malachi and Pearlbee Washington. As proud as any father, Malachi patted Molly's hand wrapped around his arm, and Pearlbee, smiling out at the crowd, nodded greetings.

Molly's loving gaze met Orie's. He returned it. Eager to get to the gazebo, Molly took too long a stride. She stepped on her dress hem and staggered forward. Gasps went up from the fearful crowd. The bride was going to fall on her face. Malachi reached out and caught her. The look of consternation on Molly's face was replaced with a slight smile when she looked at Orie again. He nodded his encouragement to keep coming.

The bride looked pleased by the decorations adorning the gazebo. Once again her steps faltered. She stared at the rose bushes surrounding the gazebo. The red and white rose bushes bloomed profusely, but the pink rose bushes were all leaves and bare stems. For the first time, Gracie realized what was wrong. A rose eating insect, if there was such a thing, couldn't have done a better job of stripping the flowers from those stark stems. Molly frowned. Again, the bridegroom sensed that his bride was unhappy. He smiled and nodded at her. Her face became serene again. Her concern forgotten, she focused on the gazebo door Malachi held open for her.

Gracie whispered over her shoulder to Sara, "Who scalped the pink flowers off those bushes?"

Sara looked uneasy. "I hope that Molly isn't too upset. Uncle Malachi cut them for us to use on the gazebo decorations."

"Why would he do a dumb thing like that?"

"Moxie told him to. We couldn't buy as many pink roses as we needed. She said there's still plenty of red and white roses left on the other bushes to look good."

Shaking her head at how Moxie thought, Gracie wondered how much of a shortage there would have been if Sara hadn't used so many in that funeral wreath around her neck. She turned back to concentrate on the minister when she heard him began the nuptials. "We are gathered here today to join this couple in holy matrimony."

Gracie's mind wandered to what it would have been like if she had accepted a proposal from Millard. No, she had to stop those thoughts. She was beginning to think as fickled as Melinda. Must be the day rubbed off on her. She needed to get back to reality. She had never been serious about Millard. Certainly his fine pair of horses hadn't been enough reason to run off with him. Besides Pa needed her. She had no choice but to take care of her father.

The preacher say, "If anyone has just cause why these two people should not be joined together in holy matrimony let

65

them speak now or forever hold their peace."

A woman's piercing scream tore through the crowd from the far end of Gracie's row. One by one, people jumped up, yelling at the top of their lungs. In a dominoes effect, chairs flew over backwards, clattering into the next row of guests. In turn, those chairs fell into the next row.

Hearing a loud gasp, Gracie looked toward the gazebo. A horrified look distorted Molly's face. Her hands plastered to her cheek to hold her head up. *Why, she's thinking that all these folks are standing up because they don't want her to marry Mr. Orie,* thought Gracie. *That surely couldn't be what all the fuss is about. Could it?*

Gracie leaned forward to look around Melinda and Jeffrey at the bedlam. Guests jumped up and toppled over each other's collapsing chairs. Just as the problem came past Jeffrey's feet. A small, gray blur, streaked close to the ground and raced in front of Melinda. She squealed and pressed her skirt to her, stepping quickly backward into her chair. She lost her balance. Melinda and the chair fell into Mayor Long's lap in the row behind her. The mayor's chair collapsed sideways. Mayor Long and Melinda landed in a heap on the ground with the chair on top of them. The rabbit scampered under Gracie's skirt. Before she could move, it lightly tromped her feet and scurried on its way across the yard with a flash of its white tail.

Jeffrey rushed to help Melinda. While his back was turned, a brown and white beagle dashed between his legs. Yipping in hot pursuit, the dog trailed of the rabbit. The forty pound brown and white missile bumped Jeffrey at high speed. The man lost his balance and tumbled onto a screaming Mrs. Harris, knocking her to the ground with him.

Intent on catching his prey, the beagle kept going. The rabbit skimmed under Libby and dashed beneath the piano.

66

Libby felt her skirt swish, but she was preoccupied with the commotion among the guests. She didn't realize the rabbit ducked under the piano. However, she did see the beagle coming at her. She yipped louder than the dog and tucked her skirt about her legs. Raised her feet onto the bench, she gave the canine room to belly under her. Libby yelled for the dog to go away. That had no affect on him. The beagle crouched down to sniff the underside of the piano in the direct vicinity of the rabbit's hiding place. Libby snatched her songbook and began to beat the exposed portion of the canines brown and white backside. Yipping in pain, the beagle curled his tail between his legs and backed out from under Libby's bench. He froze, looking at the noisy crowd in front of him. Bypassing the guest with a wide berth, he disappeared through the hedge. Libby slumped on the bench, weakly fanning herself to keep from fainting.

The bride opened the gazebo door. She looked concerned. "I'm sorry for this unexpected interruption. I do hope that no one was hurt, but I'm glad you're not all standing to bear witness that Orie and I should not be married. You had me worried for a moment."

Laughing at Molly's mistaken concern, the guests chattered about such an unexpected turn of events at a wedding. Orie, Earl and the minister rushed out of the gazebo to help the guests upright their chairs into orderly rows, checking as they went to make sure no one was hurt.

Once all the guests settled back in their uprighted chairs, Orie rejoined Molly in front of the minister again with Earl by his side. "Let's go on with this wedding. I've waited long enough," said the bridegroom in a loud voice, causing titters among the guests.

Gracie fumed silently through the rest of the ceremony.

Of all days for that beagle to get loose. Why did he have to pick this one? It'd be just like those Maudie's ruffians to let that dog go on purpose. Those Brown younguns, with red haired, freckle faced Tommy leading the pack, might be standing behind the hedge, watching that mutt interrupt the wedding. If she could have left the ceremony, she'd stab a stick through a few of the bushes just to see if she could roust them ornery boys out. She did that before when she caught Tommy hid out in there, throwing rocks at a passerby's horse. Maudie Brown's brood was nothing but trouble, and Tommy was the instigator.

"Now I pronounce you man and wife. Ladies and gentlemen, may I present to you Mr. and Mrs. Orie Lang. You may kiss the bride, Orie," finished the preacher.

Orie give Molly a peck on the mouth. She cupped his face in her hands and gave him a big, long kiss. Orie blushed. Molly's loud, happy laughter rang out.

"Follow us to the reception table," invited the bride, walking by the rows of chairs to the table.

On one end was a crystal, punch bowl full of pink punch and stacks of dainty, glass cups. The kind of cup that Gracie was pretty sure a body had to hold with their little finger stuck out. Next to the punch sat the three tiered, wedding cake, a tiny bride and groom perched on top surrounded by pink roses with green leaves. Molly picked up the knife. With Orie's hand over hers, they sliced through the bottom tier. As Molly pried up on the piece, a series of loud honks came from the northern skyline. She looked up. "Geese going over. Look how low they're flying. They know winter's coming. Aren't they lovely to watch?"

Gracie watched the v formation above her. It was easy to make out their gray bellies, and outstretched black necks. How wildly graceful they flew, gliding over the wedding party and the reception table.

A soft plunk caused Molly to gasped. Gracie followed the bride's horrified gaze to the punch bowl. A wave of pink punch slopped over the edge of the bowl. It cascade down the side and soaked into the white, linen tablecloth, slowly spreading pink stain into a large circle around the bottom of the bowl. A mysterious lump floated in the punch, rocking in waves created by its free fall like a log on the Iowa River. A mixture of white and green, the lump slowly dissolved in the bowl while it drifted in the ripples.

Horrified, Molly looked from Gracie to Sara. The three of them darted a glance around to see if any of the guests noticed this newest, embarrassing moment for Molly's wedding. She lamented just above a whisper, "I don't believe this. What is going to go wrong next?"

"It's all right, Molly. I'll get a fresh bowl. Aunt Pearlbee made plenty," Sara assured her. "Everyone's so busy talking, they didn't see what happened. Just go on feeding Orie the cake. I'll be right back with another bowl of punch."

Sara took off with the bowl partially hidden in her rose necklace."Where you going with the punch?" asked Earl when Sara walked slowly past him, trying not to spill punch on her dress. "I wanted a cup of it."

"Not so loud," Sara hissed. "A goose pooped in it," she whispered in Earl's ear.

"Well, that bird must be right proud of himself. He has mighty good aim," replied Earl, cracking himself up. He sobered when Sara gave him a dagger filled look that could have killed.

She nodded toward the distraught bride. "I'm sorry about Earl, Molly. Truly I am."

Gracie wanted to grin, but not with Melinda beside her.

69

She knew that would get her Melinda's elbow in the ribs. She couldn't help identifying with Earl. Nothing wrong with a sense of humor about things that happen that you can't do anything to prevent.

After the cake cutting, Melinda seized the opportunity to introduce Jeffrey to the newlyweds. "Congratulations to you both," he said, extending his hand to them.

"It's so nice to meet you," said Molly. "We're glad that you could come to spend the day with your aunt."

"Not just for the day, ma'am. I'd like to stick around awhile. Get to know Aunt Melinda better," declared Jeffrey, looking questioningly at his aunt.

"Oh how wonderful," gushed Melinda. She hugged the young man's arm.

Gracie didn't like the happy expression on Melinda's face. She wished her friend would be more cautious about this stranger. It'd be advisable for Melinda to make sure Jeffrey Armstrong was who he said he was before she got so attached to him. Maybe she best mention that to Melinda the first time they had a few moments alone.

Chapter 10

Orie helped Molly into his buggy, He made several tries to fold in the volumes of white satin that kept billowing out toward him before he succeeded. "See you all out at the farm in a little while for the dance," he called, waving at the crowd while he whipped the horses reins.

The buggy traveled slowly down the street. A string of tin cans, attached to the back, rattled and bounced. At the end of the string, a pair of old high top farmer shoes trailed along in the dust followed by a pair of light green heels with scalloped tops. Those heels looked familiar to Gracie, but she couldn't remember where she'd seen them. Dang her memory. Maybe it'd come to her later like every other delayed thought she'd had lately.

It felt good to sit down in the parlor and finally relax now that the wedding was over. Nothing to do but wait until time to leave for Orie's farm. A long evening promised to stretch out ahead of Gracie. She'd already had enough of a day. She felt weary just thinking about the barn dance. Instead, she tried to focus on the prattle going on between Moxie and Melinda about the wedding, but her thoughts kept going back to Jeffrey Armstrong. The man was wedged between his aunt and Moxie on the settee. Relaxed back with his lengthy legs stretched out, he seemed content. A rather pleasant looking young man, Gracie had to admit even though his eyes shifted way too fast, taking in everything all at once. It might be easier for her to get use to him being around if he didn't act so suspicious.   Underneath that placid exterior, he acted edgy enough to make her think the devil himself was after the man.

"Ladies, please excuse me. I want to go to the water closet before we leave," Jeffrey said, standing up.

"We all should think about that, shouldn't we, Gracie?" asked Melinda.

Gracie didn't hear her. Jeffrey turned the wrong way down the hall toward the outside door. Perhaps he didn't know his way about, but if he didn't know the way to the water closet, why hadn't he asked? Jeffery Armstrong didn't appear to be the bashful type to her. She stared at the doorway, waiting for him realize his mistake and come back by.

"Gracie, don't you think we should think about leaving soon? Gracie, are you listening to me?" persisted Melinda.

"What?" Gracie asked absently, not taking her eyes from the door. It had been too long now. Jeffrey had to realize his mistake. "Oh, I'm ready whenever the rest of you are." She rubbed her arms. "I feel a bit chilly. I think I left my shawl out on the hall table. I'll go get it."

"All right, dear," said Melinda. "Miss Moxie and I'll wait here for you and Jeffrey."

Jeffrey wasn't in the hall. Perhaps he decided to leave without saying anything. That would disappoint poor Melinda if he decided to change his mind about taking them to the barn dance. Gracie picked up her shawl. She draped it around her shoulders and started back past the library. Puzzled that the door was shut, she stop.   No one ever shut that door. She placed her hand on the knob, giving it a gentle twist. She pushed the door open a crack and peeked in.

Standing on a chair in front of the book shelves, Jeffrey pulled a book out of the top shelf. He opened it and flipped through a few pages. Closing it, he slipped the book inside his suit jacket and stepped down from the chair. Gracie eased the door shut as fast as she could and hurried to take her seat in the parlor. What on earth was that man doing? If he wanted to read a book why didn't he just say so? He lied about where he was going. He shut the library door so no one would see what he did. He stole one of Miss Molly's books, but he didn't know much about priceless books. That brown covered book wasn't one of the first additions so why would he want it?

Deep in thought, Gracie flinched at the sound of Jeffrey's voice when he burst back into the parlor, announcing he was ready to leave.

"Are you still cold now since you got your shawl from the hall table, Gracie? If so you best bundle up good for the ride out to Mr. Orie's farm. We need to get our coats. It'll be cold tonight when we start home," instructed Melinda.

Gracie glanced at Jeffrey. He stared at her with a smoldering expression on his face and one eyebrow raised. "Maybe Miss Gracie hasn't had time to warm up, Aunt Melinda. When did she get her shawl?" He asked, not taking his eyes off Gracie.

"Just a few minutes ago," cheeped the little lady.

"Is that right? I do hope you've warmed up by now," Jeffrey said. His voice was icy sounding through tightened lips.

"I'm fine," returned Gracie calmly, thinking some things never change. Melinda always talked when she should keep her mouth shut.

Jeffrey seemed to relax again. Maybe he decided she hadn't seen anything with the door shut. She hoped that was the case. The young man glanced around the parlor. "Where's Miss Libby?"

"She's not going with us," Melinda said and sighed. "I tried to tell her she'd miss a good time, but she wouldn't consent to go."

"Of course not. Heaven forbid, she have a good time for once in her life," groused Gracie.

"Now, now, Gracie, be nice," cooed Melinda. "Libby can stay home if she wants to."

"I reckon that's true. I have half a mind to stay home myself," confessed Gracie, thinking she'd be better off staying away from Melinda's nephew for a while.

"You will not. I won't hear of it. Libby not going is one thing, but Miss Molly wants you at her barn dance. Now go get your coat on. Let's go to a the party," ordered Melinda with a big grin.

Jeffrey helped Gracie onto the back seat of the buckboard. She didn't dare look at him for fear he'd sense she'd seen him in the library. The young man assisted Melinda up to the front seat and climbed up beside her. He clicked to the horses, and they were off to the barn dance.

They had a half hour ride ahead of them. Time to reminisce while Gracie listened to the steady clop of horse hooves as the buckboard creaked over the rough road. They'd pass her farm on the way to Orie's place. Since she hadn't seen it for so very long, she would have liked to see the place in the daylight. A sad nostalgia crept over her. She missed calling it home. After all, she'd spent the better part of her life there until she moved into the Moser Mansion.

In a short time, Gracie stretched up and patted Melinda on the back. "That's my farm, Three Oaks."

In the dusk, large shadows loomed against the skyline, but Gracie imagined that things didn't look much different from the way she remembered them. The house's clapboard had turned a soft gray over the years. The barn and outbuildings weathered to a dark gray with rusting, tin roofs. The large silhouettes in the front yard were oak trees that shaded the house from the west sun. An ancient burr oak stood in the barn yard. Back of the barn, corn shocks loomed black against the horizon like a village of Indian tepees. That's the way she remembered the place in fall when she'd looked around her in satisfaction at completing harvest. *Reckon I can still call that place home whether I live there or not.* She folded her arms over her chest to keep the shawl from flapping open in the breeze.

Jeffrey pulled the buckboard into Orie's driveway and halted the team by the barn. On one side of the buckboard was the one story house. On the other side sat the red barn, impressive compared to the small one on Gracie's farm. Under the eve, 1889 was painted in white on the red boards. That was date that the barn was built. Fairly new barn compared to some in the area. That large a barn must be a sign that Orie was a successful farmer. That was good for Miss Molly's future well being.

Lanterns hooked to the barn, swayed gently in the breeze, lighting a broad jittery swath of light. The ladder rose steeply up to the loft opening. The ascent suddenly seemed akin to a mountain climbing task, but Gracie was determined to give it a try. She grabbed the railing and gathered a hand full of skirt, tightening the material around her legs to keep the breeze from blowing under. She didn't want to expose her bloomers to the men standing around. She looked around her to see how close any male guests might be.

"Oh, Gracie, just go, will you? I hear music. I want to get to the dance," grumped Melinda, giving her a shove in the back.

"If you're in such a hurry you go first," offered Gracie, stepping out of the way.

With a slight quirk at the corners of his mouth, Jeffrey

came to Gracie's rescue whether she wanted him to or not. "Ladies, please let me escort you one at a time up the ladder. It'd be my pleasure to help you, Aunt Melinda. I'll come back down for you next, Miss Gracie."

"That's a great idea, Jeffrey. Thank you so much." Melinda started up the ladder with her nephew right behind her. Gracie stood with her hands on her hips, marveling at the youthful spring Melinda developed in her climb with the anticipation of dancing.

After depositing Melinda through the narrow, loft door, Jeffrey, taking two steps at a time, came back down the ladder. "Now it's your turn, Miss Gracie."

"I'll have you know most likely I've climbed into more hay lofts in my time than you have at your age. Mostly for the hard work of putting up hay and throwing fork fulls back down to feed instead of this foolishness. Reckon I can make it up to the loft this time, too," Gracie barked.

"I'm sure you can, but let a gentleman do the honor of escorting you, please Miss Gracie," he begged as if he meant it, beaming what looked like a friendly smile at her.

Gracie took another look up the steep incline. She hesitated, thinking about her bum knee. This city slicker's help was probably safer than trying to climb up the ladder by herself. Besides if she fell on him that would be a softer landing. She nodded at him, grabbed the rail, and a handful skirt. Gracie climbed slowly one step at a time, feeling a twinge in her knee. The newly made steps smelled of sawed wood and seemed quite sturdy, but Gracie dared not inspect Orie and Malachi's handwork too closely as she inched farther away from the ground.

"You're doing fine, Miss Gracie," came the smooth male voice behind her.

Gracie's hand gripping the rail trembled. She didn't know if the shakiness was from holding on so tight or knowing that this strange man was close behind her. She tried to steady herself.

Jeffrey's strong hand darted from behind and clamped on hers. "Steady, Miss Gracie, you wouldn't want to fall. It's a long ways down," he said coolly.

"Take your hand off me. I can make it," Gracie bit at him.

He removed his hand. "Of course, you'll make it. If you don't mind me saying so just watch your step real careful like. You never know what can happen when you're not careful," Jeffrey warned.

Had that man just threatened her or was she imagining things? Climbing faster, Gracie kept her eyes on the loft opening, concentrating into the watchful faces of Sara, Earl and Melinda.

"Step on up here, Miss Gracie," Sara urged, still wearing her slightly wilted rose necklace.

Earl offered her a hand to steady her until she was solid on her feet. "You're on solid flooring now."

Melinda praised, "Good job, Gracie."

"I'm up here now, but sooner or later, I have to make the trip back down those steps. I sure hoped I'm up to it," Gracie grumped.

Melinda giggled. "Oh, Gracie, you wouldn't be Gracie if you didn't worry about something." She turned her attention from Gracie to the music that had been playing while they climbed up to the loft. She began to tap her foot in time to the music.

A four man band, three fiddlers and an accordion player, stood in one corner of the loft in front of a mound of hay, tuning up for the first dance. They practiced "Red Wing". The accordion player belted out loud and clear, "The moon shines on the shy little prairie maid as she weeps through the night, mourning the loss of her beloved warrior brave."

It had been a long time since Gracie heard that sad song about a broken hearted Indian maiden, but she remembered it with a combination of pleasure and melancholy. The song brought memories of barn lofts and other dances flooding back to her. shiny floors, swept clean in the middle and polished slick from the many feet that shuffled on those boards. Lined up along the walls, foot boards perched on tin buckets turned upside down made seats for the guests to rest on between dances. Lanterns hung on nails high above the seats. The scene hadn't changed any after all those years. *Just my age,* thought Gracie.

People mingled in groups, chatting in the glow from the lanterns. They waited for all the guests to arrive so the dance could begin. Orie had nailed up a large board with the words painted on it, "No Smoking in the Loft." *Good idea,* Gracie agreed. Orie didn't want his fine barn burnt to the ground. A careless toss of a smoldering match into the dry hay could send the building up in flames. Maybe a bunch of people, too. Not many folks would be able to make it down those narrow steps at once. With as slow as she was, Gracie was certain she wouldn't be one of the lucky ones to get out of the barn.

Sara handed Gracie a dance card.

"What am I suppose to do with this?"

Sara grinned at her. "Hang on to it. You might get lucky."

It had been so long that Gracie had forgotten about that little detail. At her age, she didn't figure on filling it. The small piece of paper had two numbered row on which men could write in their names for a certain dance. Below each line was written whether the dance would be a two step, waltz or polka which came in handy for the gentlemen who were better at one kind of dance then another. Good idea for the ladies, too. *It'd keep them from getting their toes tromped on so much,* ran through Gracie's mind. She grinned at the idea of clumsy farmers standing on the toes of the ladies fancy shoes.

"May I have the honor of signing your dance card, Miss Gracie," asked Jeffrey.

"What?" Deep in thought, it took Gracie a minute to register what the young man said. "This thing? Don't know if I want to dance yet."

"Please give me the honor. I just signed Aunt Melinda's, and I want to dance with you, too," he wheeled.

"Fine! Sign it but if I change my mind you'll just have to dance with someone else." If he thought he could sidle up to her just because he was Melinda's nephew, he better think again. She still wasn't convinced that she liked this stranger especially since he made that crack about watching her step while they were coming up the ladder. She didn't feel the need to get too friendly just yet.

The fiddlers began to play for real this time. Holding hands, Molly and Orie walked out to the middle of the loft. Lovingly, the bride and groom looked into each other's eyes, slowly dancing a two step. The tune changed. Moxie accompanied by Earl joined the newlyweds for the next dance. As soon as that dance was over, there was a pause before the next one began.

Jeffrey headed over toward Gracie, Melinda and Moxie. Gracie held her breath for fear that he'd have the nerve to ask her to dance. She breathed a sigh of relief when he stopped in front of Melinda.

79

"Aunt Melinda, may I have the honor of this dance?"

"I'd be delighted kind sir," she replied.

Gracie grimaced at all the formality. It was a game she wasn't prepared to play. *Such foolishment,* she scoffed to herself.

When the music stopped, Jeffrey escorted Melinda back to the empty space beside Gracie. He turned to Moxie and offered her his hand. With a dreamy look on her face, Melinda watched the young couple waltz around the floor. She turned to Gracie. "Jeffrey is such a good dancer. Don't you think he and Miss Moxie make a cute couple?"

"Miss Moxie's too short for that man," Gracie said bluntly.

"Just the same they're about the same age and seem to get along well together," insisted Melinda.

"Didn't notice."

Undaunted by Gracie's abruptness, Melinda, her eyes sparkling, continued, "Wouldn't it be grand if Jeffrey and Miss Moxie hit it off, and he decided to stay in Locked Rock. I'd have a relative near me all the time."

This was the moment that Gracie had been waiting for. She had to try to get through to Melinda again. "He don't look like the kind that'd stay put for very long. I wouldn't get your hopes already up if I were you," she warned. Besides, Melinda, you ought to go slow with that young man. You don't know anything about him, and he don't look to me like the kind that stays put very long." There she'd said it. Not that it did her any good. Melinda focused on the dancers like she hadn't been listening to Gracie.

As green as Moxie was, Gracie feared that young girl getting interested in Jeffrey could only lead to getting her heart broke. That tall, good looking man was too much of a charmer to be true. Gracie was sure of that. He reminded her of Dan Jordan their former neighbor, the duded up salesman. One day, the man packed a valise and walked away from his wife. No, it was more like he ran, but Gracie hardly blamed him. His wife, Mavis, turned out to be a murderer. Still in all, he had the same kind of shiftless charm Gracie saw in Melinda's nephew. A suspicious thought crossed her mind about what dire circumstances might be in that young man's background. He seemed too nervous to her, always watchful of everyone around him. Who was he always looking for, or who didn't he want to see him?

Involuntarily tapping her foot to the lilt of the fiddle music, Gracie listen to the whisper of the many feet shuffling along on the slick, loft floor. She began to relax just when the music stopped. The dancers parted. Gracie stiffened. A vaguely familiar, older, short man headed toward her. She watched him come. She could be wrong but that old man looked a little like Millard Sokol. Could it be possible he came to this dance? If she'd thought that could happen, she wouldn't have showed up. She hadn't seen for him in years. She didn't want to now. The man closed the distance between them. When he got close, she knew for sure it was Millard. He hadn't changed much, still short and homely, and considerable older. She couldn't fault him for that since that description fit her as well.   Furtively, Gracie searched for a place to hide in the crowd. By that time Millard was so close, she knew she'd never be fast enough to get up and lost with her bum knee. She looked away from him, hoping he change directions. No such luck. Millard Sokal stopped right in front of her.

She studied the scuff toes of his high top farmer shoes to keep from looking up at him. He spoke softly in that gravel voice of his, "Evening, Miss Gracie. How you been?"

81

"All right," she muttered, looking around from under her ducked head to see who might be paying attention to their exchange right into the curious eyes of Melinda.

"You remember me, do ya?" asked Millard Sokol, clearing his throat.

Gracie looked at him. "Yip, I recollect who you are. How you been, Millard?" She asked, dully.

"Right fine. I wondered if you'd do me the honor of this dance, Miss Gracie?" Millard asked, shifting from one foot to the other.

"No," she said, her mind rushing for a escape plan. She spied Jeffrey. He returned Moxie to her seat and leaned against the wall beside her. "Someone already signed my dance card for this dance." Standing up too fast, Gracie wobbled. She steadied herself and hobbled over to Jeffrey. Not the least bit sorry to interrupt the young couple, Gracie stated, "Time for that dance.

Jeffrey came away from the wall. "Really Miss Gracie?"

"You're the one that signed this, ain't you?" Gracie waved the dance card in his face.

"Oh yes, ma'am, I surely did. I'd be honored," he said, grinning. "Excuse us, Miss Moxie. I'll be back shortly to have another dance with you." He escorted Gracie to the dance floor and held his arms out for her to step into them.

The music started. Gracie let him turn her onto the dance floor. She looked back to find Millard, his arms folded across his chest, watching her. She could only hope that he'd move on before the dance was over. Since no one else had asked her to dance, Gracie didn't have another escape plan. She wasn't too crazy about going back to sit near Millard. The man had a speculative look on his face, and he didn't seem to be in any hurry to move from that spot. Gracie felt her heart sink into her stomach as she watched Millard sit down next to Melinda and speak to her. The little lady nodded at him and smiled that too sweet smile of hers.

Jeffrey moved Gracie so that her back was to what was happening. She looked up at Jeffrey's face. He hadn't said a word since they started dancing. He seemed to be concentrating more on the crowd then he was the dance. Gracie followed his gaze to a group of men, talking in one corner. Jeffrey studied first one of the men then another with an speculative intense stare.

Curious, Gracie asked, "See anyone you know, Mr. Armstrong?"

"What?" He asked, startled by Gracie's question. He recovered quickly. Chuckling, he said lamely, "Oh, no, just studying the competition, Miss Gracie."

If he thought those old codgers were his competition with her, Gracie didn't find that one bit funny. She was ready to tell him so when he turned her toward Melinda and Millard again. They were laughing. What could Millard have said to her that was so dang funny. This dance couldn't last very much longer. It looked as if Millard had settled into her spot for the duration of the evening. If Gracie intended to go back to that spot to sit, she'd have to do it with him still there. Not only was he in no hurry to leave, he seemed to be having a good time talking to Melinda. Why she even looked like she was flirting with him. That Melinda never knew when to keep her mouth shut. Gracie didn't know which was worse. Melinda flirting with Millard, or the Melinda was telling him something about her.

The music stopped. Jeffrey took his bowler off and made a wide sweeping bow. "Thank you so much for the

83

honor, Miss Gracie. I do hope this means that we are becoming friendly."

"Don't get carried away, young man. It just means that you were better than the alternative," she snapped. She didn't wait to see what he thought of that remark. She had to head back over to where Millard sat with Melinda. She figured she better break those two up before they did too much reminiscing about her.

Millard rose to greet her. "Well, Miss Gracie, would you do me the honor of the next dance?"

"Reckon, I'll set this one out. I'm ready to rest a spell," she excused, remembering to make more of an effort to limp. "Have a bum knee that acts up if I'm on my feet too long." She sat down and rubbed her knee vigorously to cement the statement.

Melinda started, "Gracie, surely you could ... ."

"I said I needed to rest," Gracie snapped. she raised the paper fan she hung onto from the reception up to her right cheek and rubbed it against a nervous itch.

"I reckon I'll just join you then if you don't mind. Like to talk a spell." Before she could object, he sat down beside her, stretched his legs out, crossing them at the ankles. "Don't this here dance remind you of all them years ago when we used to go dancing together."

"Not really. Hadn't give it much thought. That was a long time ago. I was younger then. Took more of a liking to such foolishness than I should have." Gracie whipped her fan in front of her face. Bringing the fan up by her right ear, she scratched the back of her neck to stop a trickle of sweat.

"Reckon I could say the same thing. Of course, I kept in better shape as far as dancing was concerned when my wife, Addie, was alive. She did love to dance. Since her passing, I

84

don't partake in dances anymore." With a sad, lonesome look on his face, he stared off across the crowded dance floor.

"How come you're here then?" asked Gracie, looking down at her lap as she digested the fact that Millard was a widower.

"I work back and forth with Orie. Our farms join. I didn't think it'd be right for me not to show up tonight with him getting married and all."

I suppose not." Gracie gave him a new once over. She had to admit he was thoughtful to come. Now that she took the time to think about it, Millard cleaned up right nice for an old man. He smelled of pipe smoke, but that wasn't so bad. The smell reminded her of her father. It strayed through her mind to wonder if he still had a nice pair of horses to pull his buggy. Now why had she bothered to think about any of this. The music must be making her moon struck as Melinda. She had to stop wondering anything that had to do with this old man beside her.

Gracie scooted closer to Melinda. she swished the fan back and forth and covered her face while she yawned. "Reckon it's about my bedtime."

"You might be right. Reckon I best think about going for home," said Millard, opening his pocket watch to check the time. I have to be up early in the morning to finish up the corn picking. I'm almost done. Nice talking to you, Miss Gracie." He stood up and twisted to add, "I'll be seeing you around … maybe."

Gracie thought she heard a touch of hopefulness in the man's voice. She chided herself for hearing things that weren't there. "Sure thing, maybe," she said shortly, looking at the floor to keep from meeting his gaze.

"He seems like a nice man," suggested Melinda. She

85

watched the farmer walk toward the loft opening. "How come you never told me about him before?"

"I did mention him to you. Once on the porch when you asked me why I never married. Just not by name."

"Oh, he's the one. There must be more to this story," pried Melinda.

"Didn't figure there was much to tell. That was a long time ago," Gracie said abruptly, hoping to put an end to the conversation.

"Looks to me like there's more to tell than you're letting on from what Mr. Sokol told me. You certainly were saying plenty with that fan in the last few minutes. Did you know there's a code of messages that goes with the way you move that fan?"

"It's hot in here. I don't know anything about messages. Just trying to cool off," defended Gracie.

"Didn't look like it to me?" teased Melinda with a glint of humor lighting up her eyes.

"What did I do?"

"When you placed the fan behind your neck, you said, "Don't forget me.""

"I sure wouldn't say that. I don't expect Millard Sokol has thought much about me since he married another woman."

"His wife died," Melinda reminded her and continued, "When you rubbed your fan on your right cheek you said yes, and if you had placed it on the left cheek you'd have been signaling no."

"Well, I surely hope I said yes and no in the right places," quipped Gracie.

Melinda paused while she tried to recall. "I'm not sure now. The best part was when you covered up your eyes with the fan. You signaled I love you."

"Now I know you're pulling my leg. I did no such thing. Besides I didn't know anything about fan messages."

"You better hope that Mr. Sokol didn't get the wrong impression then," Melinda suggested with a tongue in cheek grin.

Gracie frowned at a sprig of hay, she nudged around on the slick floor with the toe of her high top shoe. "Not much chance he knows anymore about what you're talking about then I do. He's just a farmer."

"A special farmer from your past, the way he tells it," said Melinda with a grin.

"Don't pay any never mind to what that man says. There wasn't much to remember. I promise you that," declared Gracie, frowning at the dancers for a moment. Finally, her curiosity got the better of her. She twisted toward Melinda. "What did he say anyway?"

"Oh nothing you'd want to hear, I guess," said Melinda, nonchalantly as she watched the dancers.

Now she decides not to talk. Gracie wanted to know yet she was afraid to push Melinda for more information. Deep down, she was afraid of what she'd hear.

Chapter 11

Early the next morning, a succession of loud, brassy noises woke Gracie up. At first, she couldn't figure out what made that strange racket, then she remembered the telephone. She mumbled, "That contraption's going to be on its way out the door if folks think they can call any time they want." The nerve of whoever it was, waking her up after she'd had very little sleep. She'd have a talk with Miss Molly about getting rid of the telephone. Then she remembered Molly was on her honeymoon. It would be a month before she'd be back. Whether Gracie liked it or not, she'd be putting up with that noisy interrupter for a long time.

Gracie rubbed her gritty eyes and tried to go back to sleep. She couldn't. She might as well get up. She took her sweet time getting dressed, not caring if she was late to breakfast. In fact, she noted she was the last one when she entered the kitchen. Everyone, with glum looks on their faces, watched Gracie sit down. Not one good morning in the bunch of them, but Gracie didn't really care. She wasn't in any mood to return the greeting if there had been one.

It soon became apparent what the long faces were all about. Moxie had already made an announcement to the other residents. She repeated it to Gracie. "Agnes Barnes rang up on the telephone."

"So that's who woke me up," growled Gracie. "Someone needs to talk to Agnes about how early she can call on that contraption."

Moxie ignored Gracie's complaint. "Sure and she had

an important message this mornin'. she's sick so she won't be able to do the house cleaning so ..."

Gracie butted in. "What's Agnes's ailment?

Moxie said, "She didn't say, and I didn't ask, but ..."

"She appeared to be having a good time last night at the barn dance. Maybe she enjoyed herself a little too much," Gracie suggested, between blowing on her hot coffee.

Moxie took a deep breath and started again, "Never the less, Miss Gracie. I'm charge while Molly's on her honeymoon. I can't leave the mansion in a state of disarray now that the wedding tis over. If ye ladies would be so kind, ye need to help dust and clean."

Gracie dropped her coffee cup, creating a puddle under it. She looked from Melinda to Libby. They both nodded quietly to confirm Moxie told them the same thing. Gracie

Oblivious to what passed between the residents, Moxie assigned, "Miss Gracie, ye can dust the parlor and dining room. Then sweep the floors. Miss Libby and Miss Melinda, please do the same in all the upstairs rooms. Aunt Pearlbee will in charge of cleaning the kitchen."

"What are you going to do?" asked Gracie.

"I've some errands to run. I'll be back in time for lunch. Carry on and do the good job I know ye can," she said over her shoulder, hurrying out of the kitchen.

"Errands my foot. Her errand is probably 6 feet tall with two legs and answers to the name of Jeffrey," grumbled Gracie.

"Now, now, Gracie it won't hurt us to help out once until Agnes gets back on her feet," replied Melinda.

"I planned to finish reading a book I put down until the wedding was over," fretted Libby. When she met Melinda's frowning gaze, she relented, "Guess it will wait a little longer."

At lunch time, Gracie met the others in the kitchen. She

flopped into her chair, complained, "I never seen the like. We're doing all the work here while Miss Moxie's off enjoying herself. I realized Miss Molly had put that girl in charge, but I don't think Molly meant for Miss Moxie to turn us into slave laborers just cause we live her." Pearlbee slammed a kettle down on the work counter. That silenced Gracie. The cook stood with her hands on her hips, giving Gracie a wild eyed stare. "No offense, Aunt Pearlbee. Reckon, I'm just tired," apologized Gracie. She decided she better give the subject of house cleaning a rest and tackle her lunch before Pearlbee took it away from her.

Lunch was almost over when Moxie burst into the kitchen.

"Hello, Miss Moxie. We've been wondering where you were. You almost missed lunch," replied Melinda.

"Get them errands done," snapped Gracie

"Yes, thank ye," Moxie replied sheepishly.

"Glad to hear it. *We* got all the housework done. Now, Boss, this afternoon if you haven't any other orders for us, we intend to take it easy," grumped Gracie.

"I'm going to take a nap. I don't want to be disturbed for the rest of the afternoon," declared Libby, sounding very much like she meant every word.

"Sounds like a good idea to me," stated Melinda. "I'm already tired enough to sleep on a train track. I'm not use to working anymore."

"Neither is Miss Moxie if you ask me," snapped Gracie.

Moxie sat down at the table and looked at each of the women. "Faith and be glory, Miss Molly would be proud of ye. I made a pass through the rooms. The mansion looks spick and span. Ye all deserve a good nap. Now, Miss Gracie, me thinks me hears displeasure in your voice. Are ye mad at me for some reason?"

Gracie sat up very straight in her chair, ready to do battle. "Just stating the truth, Miss High and Mighty."

Melinda placed her hand on Gracie's arm, getting her attention. "Gracie, listen to me. You should go rest now. I know you ...," Melinda started quietly.

Gracie shook Melinda's hand off. She stated without mercy, "No, might as well say what's on my mind. I been thinking it all morning. Miss Moxie, you've been here for several months now freeloading off Miss Molly. Don't you think it's about time you stopped bossing us around and got a job?"

Melinda looked from red faced Gracie to the downtrodden Moxie. "Gracie, really! Miss Moxie's suppose take care of the mansion while Molly's away," she defended.

Slowly shaking her head, Moxie said, "No. For sure, it's all right. Miss Gracie tis right. I have been thoughtless to stay here and not look for employment. I'll be lookin' in the morning. How does that sound?" She blinked her eyes, trying to fight back tears when she hurried from the room.

"How could you be so mean?" Melinda accused. She threw her napkin on the table and followed after Moxie.

Surprised by Melinda's defense of Moxie, Gracie turned to Libby. She gave Gracie a half grin. Was the woman tickled that Gracie had gotten herself in hot water with Melinda and Moxie? Or, did she wish she had the nerve to tell Moxie off for making them do the housework. Gracie decided she'd didn't want to find out and wind getting into an argument with Libby. She'd caused enough trouble for one time.

The next morning at breakfast, Gracie found the atmosphere mighty uncomfortable. Melinda pushed her egg around on her plate. For once, Snippy Libby kept quiet.

91

Moxie pushed her empty plate back and stated, "Well, if I be goin' job hunting this morning, I best get started."

Melinda gave Gracie a lemonade look.

Gracie figured Melinda wanted her to make amends somehow for yesterday. "Reckon I ought to go with you," she suggested.

Melinda relaxed and smiled slightly.

"Horse feathers! Sure and that isn't necessary. I can do this alone," Moxie said defensively.

"I know most everyone around here so maybe I can be of some help. I'm going with you," Gracie insisted staunchly.

Moxie gave in with a shrug of her shoulders and a quiet, "All right then."

Moxie and Gracie crossed Main street to walk by the saloon. The hitching rack was nearly always empty in the early morning hours. The fellows who frequented that place must be still sleeping, resting up for another go around tonight.

Moxie pointed. "Look there's a "Help Wanted Bar Maid" sign in the saloon window. I can try there."

With a growing feeling of trepidation, Gracie steadied the yellowed sign leaning against the smoke stained glass. "I don't think you should go in there. Miss Molly wouldn't like you going in a saloon much less working in one."

"Now a job is a job. I gave ye my word yesterday I'd find proper employment. Ye are right about me. I've been freeloading at Molly's. I should take whatever job is available to make me own way. I'm going in to apply. Ye can come with me or stay out here," Moxie maintained.

Gracie hung back. She didn't especially want to set foot in that den of inequity, but she didn't want Moxie to be in the saloon unchaperoned. She had a bad feeling if Moxie got a job as bar maid, it'd be her not Moxie that Molly would give a hard time. No matter how hard she tried to do the right thing, Gracie felt fate alway managed to step in and put her in hot water.

᠊ Gracie followed the younger woman through the batwing doors, determined to stop her somehow or other. Inhaling a breath of stale air, she gathered her shawl to her nose to breathe through it. The place reeked with the yeasty odor of stale beer spills and tobacco smoke. Unlit oil lamps with blackened glass shades hung from the rafters. The unpainted walls, dirty, bare floor and ring smudged tables didn't make an appealing place to work for a lady. That was for certain.

The barrow bellied bartender nodded at them and continued sweeping the floor. "What can I do for you ladies this morning," he grumped.

"Me sees ye have a need for a bar maid. I'd like to apply for that job" Moxie said, crisply business like.

"Somehow I don't think you'll do for the job, ma'am," said the man, looking the small woman up and down.

"Tis a very hard worker I am," replied Moxie, indignantly.

"I'm sure you are, but have you ever worked as a bar maid before?"

"No sir, but I can learn quickly what is needed I assure ye of that," insisted Moxie with confidence.

The man tilted his head over one shoulder and thought for a moment. "All right, walk over behind the bar and let's see," he invited, a wide grin spreading across his face.

A larger than life painting in a gilded frame hung high on the wall behind the bar. Gracie squinted one eye shut, but that didn't change the fact that the almost naked, young woman, lying on a bright red fainting couch, didn't seem to mind getting herself painted in that fix. At least, not if you took into account the half smile on her face. Thinking about Moxie

93

standing under that painting while she worked would be just the top of the crust in Molly's anger when she found out abut all this. All of her anger would be aimed at Gracie for starting this mess while Molly was gone on her honeymoon. Gracie groaned inwardly at the fix she was in. Molly was sure to find out. Libby would be glad to fill her in on the details if Moxie or Melinda failed to mention this.

Moxie didn't seem to notice the picture. She walked down to the end of the bar and disappeared behind it.

"You back there lady?" The bartender blustered like she had gone a block away.

Moxie stood on tiptoes. Only her eyes and nose showed. She peered over the bar at the bartender.

"See what I mean. You won't do at this time, but now of course if you was to grow another foot then you can come back and apply again," the man said. He slapped his leg and guffawed at his joke.

Relief flooded through Gracie. She wasn't going to have to make a scene after all to get Moxie to turn down the bar maid job.

Moxie's heels rapped loudly on the wood floor. She stomped past Gracie and the bartender to the swinging doors. She stopped without turning, waiting for Gracie to catch up.

"Look, ma'am, if you really need a job, we could use a piano player," the man said, pointing out the old piano and claw foot stool on the left side of the bar.

"I can't play a lick," Moxie replied sharply over her shoulder.

"Well, being short wouldn't matter if girl wanted to serve drinks and be nice to the customers in one of the rooms upstairs. If you get my drift," the bartender said, looking Moxie up and down again as if he was inspecting a horse.

"She ain't interested," growled Gracie, shoving Moxie through the doors. Gracie inhaled a deep breath of the fresh air. Without looking at Moxie and wanting to make sure the young girl didn't go back for that job, Gracie gave her opinion. She just hoped she didn't sound too gruff again. "Most girls that work in a place like that die of consumption. That's not a fit place for you. A ticket to the graveyard just like Rachel Simpson. Miss Molly would tell you that."

Moxie sighed, blinking her eyes at Gracie, "I'm thinkin' it's just as well I didn't get that job. I don't know how long I'd be able to stand the awful smell of the place."

They walked by the dress shop, Gracie pointed out a help wanted sign. Moxie admitted she didn't know how to sew. Gracie suggested that Melinda would be willing to give Moxie a few pointers. Moxie was sure she'd be so slow the dress shop would never want to hire her. She professed to being all thumbs as if Gracie didn't already know that. To herself, Gracie cursed that fancy back east school that didn't teach girls practical things along with the book learning.

The hardware store had a wanted clerk sign on the porch post. Gracie urged Moxie to see about that job. The building's dark interior took some getting use to, but a job was a job when you needed money. Besides being a hardware store clerk would be looked upon as respectable work in Miss Molly's eyes.

Gracie knew for sure that this was one store that hadn't changed its appearance in years. The place was a bit run down, but a body could get whatever they needed in that store. Wooden cabinets full of wide and narrow drawers lined one wall near the front of the store. A rickety ladder leaned against the cabinets to reach the higher drawers. In a line below the drawers were nail kegs and wash tubs with scrub boards in them. On the opposite wall were shelves full of tools such as hammers and wretches, large 3 legged iron cook pots and skillets. In front of the shelves on nails dangled horseshoes, harnesses, collars, and halters. Wooden pitchforks, brooms, sickles and scythes leaned against the wall Most of the tools, covered in a layer of dust, had a shiny spot here and there where a perspective customer fingered the merchandise.

Gracie walked carefully over the buckling hardwood floor to keep from stubbing her toe, following Moxie to the back of the store. In the dim light, they could just barely make out a man stocking shelves.

"Pardon me, sir," began Moxie.

Gracie had an uneasy feeling. The man's looked familiar. When he turned around, she felt down right queasy. She hadn't seen that lazy ex-town marshal, Loren Stevens, since the sheriff pulled him out of the hedges behind the mansion last August. That day, he was so drunk, he probably didn't even remember what happened, but Gracie wasn't about to forget. If things had turned out different, Mavis Jordan would have murdered Gracie and Melinda before Loren Stevens sobered up. With the shape he was in, he wouldn't have been able to identify who it was that had killed them. Good for nothing man. He deserved to get fired.

"What can I help you find? Hey, Miss Gracie," said Loren Stevens, grinning his crooked grin at her like they were on friendly terms.

Gracie nodded curtly. Best not be too rude to the man until Moxie got the job. It came to her she should feel sorry for that young woman if she had to work with the likes of that good for nothing man.

"I'm not after lookin' for anything. I wondered if I might apply for the job. I saw the sign out front."

Stevens scratched the side of his head and shifted his chew from one cheek to the other. "Now, Miss, I'm right sorry about that. I forgot to take that sign down. That's the job I was hired for a couple weeks ago," he applied.

"I see. Sure and it's thankin' ye I am anyway," said the disappointed Moxie. She walked back through the store.

Gracie looked up and down the street at the different stores. Not much possibility for employment at any of them. "Don't look like much to be had for work in this town right now. Let's go home. I'm tired of walking. We'll keep listening for something to turn up." She felt sorry for Moxie now that she had been so hard on her. Moxie's dejected look made Gracie want to make amends now that this morning of job seeking had failed. "Girl, could be the clerk job in the hardware store will open again in no time. That Loren Stevens never did a decent day's work in his life. Even too lazy to go out and take down the help wanted sign. He's likely to quit soon."

Moxie sighed deeply and shrugged her shoulders. "Sure and I'm after going home, Miss Gracie."

That night in the parlor, the ladies sat quietly lost in their own thoughts like it was too much effort to talk to one another. It was though the spark of their evening was missing with Molly gone.

"Praise be, me thinks I found a job. I have to go out for awhile," exclaimed Moxie. She threw the newspaper she'd been reading down on the settee and jumped up.

"Wait until morning. I'm too tired to go out in the cold tonight," grumped Gracie.

"No, I can take care of this meself." Moxie stated, hurrying from the parlor.

"Land's sakes, this time of night?" cried Melinda.

Libby, with a sour look on her face, asked, "What kind

97

of job is there she has to see about at night?"

"Only one kind I can think of. There's been an opening since Rachel Simpson was murdered," cracked Gracie.

"Stop that, Gracie. Miss Moxie would never try anything like a lady of the evening. She's a lady," protested Melinda.

"I thought I knew that, but we heard this morning that there's an opening in that line of work," replied Gracie, grimacing. She just pictured in her mind what Miss Molly would do to her if Moxie did indeed decide to take on the world's oldest profession.

"Well, if that poor daft girl does something foolish, it'll be all your fault," cried Melinda, holding her hanky to her nose.

Just like Melinda to read my mind. How does she do it? Even if Melinda was right, Gracie wasn't so sure she should take all the blame for Moxie making a bad decision. She snapped at Melinda, "How you figure that?"

"You're the one who told her to find a job."

Not much point in arguing that with fact since Melinda was right. If it was woman but Moxie, she'd have the sense to pick honorable employment, but who knows what Moxie had decided to do. Gracie worried that she might be partly to blame. She might have been too adamant about Moxie finding work. All it took was he bartender telling her the job was available to put the idea in that young woman's head. Maybe Moxie decided she was desperate enough to make her own way to take the bartender's offer. She'd gone traipsing out in the night unescorted, but Gracie wasn't about to go find her. Moxie would just have to take care of herself. All Gracie could do was worry about it through a sleepless night. If Moxie showed up in one piece by morning, she'd try to convince the girl what she had in mind wasn't a fit job for her.

Chapter 12

Mid morning the next day, Melinda's nephew arrived in a buggy he rented from Jake Myers livery. He took the porch steps two at a time. Bowing graciously, he invited Melinda to go for a ride with him. The elderly woman was thrilled at being asked. As the buggy disappeared from sight, Gracie heard Melinda's soft voice, chattering excitedly to her nephew.

Silence set in around Gracie. No one to talk to again. She sighed, studying the stilled rocker next to her. She thought her rocking alone days would be over after the wedding. A feeling of loneliness hit her. A flurry of cheeps came from a flock of sparrows on the telephone line, grouping together for the winter. *Even the birds have each other for company. Oh well, reckon I can always start twiddling my thumbs now.* Instead she settled back in her rocker, pulled the patchwork up higher and closed her eyes. Maybe a nap would help the morning pass faster.

After lunch, Melinda wiggled in the rocker next to Gracie, all bubbly talk abut her morning with Jeffrey. When Gracie could get a word in edge wise, she suggested they go for a walk. Gracie was ready for a change of scene, and she wanted to try to caution Melinda again that she should be careful as far as Jeffrey was concerned. She wasn't sure how to say what she was thinking, but there was so much about this nephew of Melinda's that they didn't know. To put it bluntly, he seemed sneaky, full of furtive glances and down right evasive when Gracie questioned him. She couldn't believe that by now Melinda hadn't realized there was something wrong with him.

Maybe she could believe it though. Melinda wanted a relative so bad, she didn't want to see anything bad about him. Maybe she wouldn't want to hear it, either.

"It's just a glorious fall day isn't it, Gracie? Today has been so much fun. What with going for that long ride. We stopped to eat a delicious lunch at Irene's Cafe in Van Horne," Melinda rambled on while they crossed the street.

"I reckon that's nice. Your nephew bought you lunch."

"Oh well, not exactly," said Melinda. She studied the vacant Jordan house.

"I thought you just said he took you out to eat?"

"Jeffrey did, but he accidentally left his billfold in his hotel room so I paid for the meals," shared Melinda. She spoke so low Gracie felt like Melinda thought she was sharing a sin she committed.

Licking her lips nervously, Gracie began, "I hate to speak ill of a relative of yours but …"

Melinda halted. She faced Gracie and interrupted in a defensive tone of voice. " Don't say anything at all. I don't want to hear it."

Gracie tried to continue, "I'm sorry, but I just have a bad feeling about that young man. I think you should know it."

Anger flared in Melinda's eyes. "You have had a bad feeling at one time or other about everyone you know including me so what's new?"

"Am I that bad?" Gracie asked, taken aback.

Melinda put her hand to her mouth. Her face filled with regret and her eyes welled up with tears. "Sometimes it seems like it to me, but I shouldn't have said that. Forgive me, Gracie. I know you mean well." She patted Gracie's arm.

"I've always known I say more than I should sometimes. You're right. I reckon I'm too plain a talker, but

Melinda, best go slow with this man. You don't know enough about Jeffrey yet. Can you be sure he is really your nephew?" The idea nagged at Gracie that Jeffrey could be an impostor. Maybe he was being evasive because he was hiding some sinister family secret. Suppose the man had done something unspeakable and was hiding from the law. Either way, whatever his problem was, Gracie didn't like his concealing information about himself that in the long run could hurt Melinda.

"I feel like he really is my nephew," said Melinda, softly.

"That might be because you want to have someone who's kin to you close by. You have to admit Jeffrey seems rather closed mouthed about himself. Has he told you anymore about his past?"

"No, he don't talk much about that," admitted Melinda.

"Don't you think it's time you started asking him some questions to pin him down. Don't you want to know more about your brother?" Gracie insisted.

"Of course, I do. I think Jeffrey will tell me more when he gets to know me better. After all, I'm a stranger to him as much as he is to me. Oh, let's just change the subject and enjoy this walk. What did you do this morning, Gracie?"

"Twiddled my thumbs," grumped Gracie.

"What! Oh my," said Melinda. She burst into laughter.

Even being honest with Melinda didn't bother her these days. She was happy and content. Watching her laugh was enough to make Gracie smile back Melinda. She did hope for Melinda's sake things stayed as wonderful as that gentle woman thought they were now.

The women crossed the street, walked back along the picket fence in front of the Moser yard, and came through the

101

gate. Louise Turner, a plump matronly woman who lived a block over, came down the porch steps to meet them.

Gracie said in a low voice, "Wonder why Louise came calling? She knows Miss Molly's on her honeymoon."

Melinda leaned over and whispered in Gracie's ear. "She's carrying one of Miss Molly's father's books. What do you suppose she doing with that? Oh my, look over there, Gracie." Melinda pointed toward a newly placed sign tacked on the telephone pole. The sign read "Locked Rock Public Library". The sign must be a joke on Miss Molly for her to find when she gets home. Gracie stepped in front of Louise and asked curtly, "Where do you think you're going with one of Miss Molly's fancy books?"

"I checked it out of the library," said Louise, holding the book close to her.

"Surely, there's been a mistake, Louise. This isn't the public library. Locked Rock doesn't have one," declared Melinda, trying to help Gracie set the woman straight.

"We do now. Right in there," said Louise pointing a short, pudgy finger back over her shoulder, "and Moxie McEntire is the librarian." She hugged the book to her to keep the women from snatching it from her and scurried away.

"We better go in and have a talk with Miss Moxie. Miss Molly isn't going to like this," declared Melinda.

"I knew that girl being in charge of the mansion was a bad idea. I tried to tell you so," grumbled Gracie. "Loaning anything to that Turner woman is a mistake. She won't even return a cup of sugar." Red faced, Gracie marched up the steps. "We have to stop Miss Moxie."

"Wait a minute. Cool off first, before you say something you'll regret," suggested Melinda, trailing along behind her.

102

"I won't regret saying anything. Miss Moxie has to take that library sign down right now," said Gracie over her shoulder as she marched down the entry hall.

⸝ Moxie sat at the writing table in the library. Maudie Brown stood beside her, holding another of the Moser books.

"Miss Moxie," began Gracie. seeing Maudie Brown had her picturing that brood of ornery younguns that belonged to Maudie. No telling what awful thing would happen to the book she'd take home. "Miss Moxie!"

"Sure and ye'll have to wait your turn, Miss Gracie. Mrs. Brown was here first," said Moxie, patronizingly.

It was clear that Maudie didn't seem in any hurry to leave. She kept talking. Gracie shifted her weight to one foot then the other becoming more impatient as the time went by. Finally, Gracie grabbed Maudie by the arm and escorted her to the door, resisting the urge to wrestle the woman for Molly's book. "Time's up Maudie. I need to talk to Miss Moxie about something important. Goodbye."

"Well, I never," snapped Maudie to Melinda as she left.

Melinda crossed the room and sat down on the red fainting couch. That was about as far way as she could get. If Melinda couldn't stop the inevitable she wanted to be out of way when Gracie lit in on Moxie.

"Saints preserve us, Miss Gracie. What is ailin' ye now?" Moxie leaned back in her chair and regarded Gracie in concern.

"What do you think you're doing here?" asked Gracie, braced for a fight with her hands on her hips.

"I was wantin' to tell ye about this as soon as I saw ye, but when I got home ye both were out for a walk." Moxie waved her hand around the room and announced, "It's me new job. I'm the town librarian now.".

"But Miss Moxie, dear, this library doesn't belong to the town. It's Miss Molly's library full of expensive first editions," stated Melinda in a tone she'd use on a child.

"Not right now. I'm after using it for the town's library. Ye see I applied for the job before the city council meeting last night."

"Thank heavens, that's where she went," breathed Melinda, Patting herself on the chest, she gave Gracie a relieved look.

"Go on with what you were saying," growled Gracie, not wanting to get distracted from the subject.

"They told me it paid $8.00 a month. The council hired me before they told me they didn't have a building or books yet. They couldn't pay me until the town had the money to build a library so I volunteered this one until the city can build one. Ye should be happy, Miss Gracie. Sure and now, I have decent employment," finished Moxie, looking pleased with herself.

"Well, you're wrong. I'm not happy at all and neither will Miss Molly be. You're going to have to find another job," ordered Gracie.

"For sure, I thought ye'd approve of me working." Moxie's shoulders sagged.

"Dear, it's just that we don't think Miss Molly would approve of you giving away her books," explained Melinda.

"Horse feathers, I'm not giving them away," said Moxie with a shake of her head, "I'm lending them out to people. Everyone has to pay $1.00 dues for two years to borrow the books. Would you two like to sign up and be members of the Locked Rock Library?" As if paying dues made her decision to loan out the books all right, Moxie looked from one of the other elderly ladies with a hopeful expression.

"Why should we pay you a dollar for what we've been getting for free? At least we can until the shelves go bare," grumped Gracie.

"Believe me, this is only temporary, ladies. The town has applied for a grant from the Andrew Carnegie foundation. With some proper fund raising to match the grant, the new library will be built and full of books. Then I'll go there. I promise," said Moxie, crossing her chest.

"How temporary?" asked Gracie, looking at the young woman sideways.

"Well, … in a couple of years maybe," drew out Moxie.

"That long! Miss Molly's only going to be gone for a month. You better rethink this job if I were you, Miss Moxie," warned Gracie. "What if some of these books don't come back or get damaged? Are you prepared to pay Miss Molly back? Those books cost a lot of money and can't be replaced if something happens to them."

"Oh, that wouldn't happen. Everyone is so glad to have a library they'll be very careful with the books. Sure and it is, I know they will," declared Moxie.

"I give up. Melinda, I'm going back out on the porch and twiddle my thumbs some more," said Gracie, throwing her hands up in the air.

"Sounds like fun. I'll join you," retorted Melinda, dryly.

Chapter 13

"I'd like to get to know you better. Sit down here and talk to me a spell," Gracie said to Jeffrey that afternoon. She patted the arm of the empty rocker beside her. "While Melinda's getting her coat why don't you fill me in on yourself, young man." Gracie began her interrogation. "You never did say where you came from."

"A small town in southern Missouri called Montevallo. It's about the size of Locked Rock," he replied brusquely, sliding into the rocker.

"Your folks still live there?"

"Yes, my father does the last I knew." The friendly tone in his voice of a moment ago vanished. His eyes filled with anger, and his face took on a hostile look just as Melinda opened the screen door. Jeffrey stood up quickly, masked the expression on his face and turned to his aunt. "We better get going so we finish dining and make it back here soon as we can. The evenings turn cool quick like. Been nice talking with you, Miss Gracie," he said sullenly, touching his fingers to his bowler brim. Placing Melinda's hand in the crook of his arm, he smiled down at her lovingly.

Gracie leaned back in her rocker, listening to thudding, horse hooves on the packed street and the creak of the slow moving buggy disappearing from sight. Silence settled around her. All she heard was the squeak of her rocker. The screen door banged. Gracie flinched. The dreamy look left her. She blinked and opened her eyes wide.

Libby picked up Melinda's wedding ring lap quilt out

of the rocker seat and sit down. "Oh, did I wake you?" She tried to sound apologetic.

"When you slam the door like that, what do you think?"

"I'm sorry."

"What do you want anyway?"

"I was thinking you might like some company now that Melinda isn't around very much. Her nephew seems like a nice young man, doesn't he?" Libby asked, trying to start a conversation while smoothing the lap quilt over her legs.

"Looks can be deceiving. There's something suspicious about that man. I can feel it," proclaimed Gracie.

Libby looked questioningly at Gracie. "What on earth makes you say that about that nice, young man?"

"The way he talks for one thing. He calls dinner lunch. That sounds like someone from back east not south. Besides when I asked him where he was from he tried to keep from telling me until I kept after him."

"Is that all? Maybe he just thought you were being nosy like usual," Libby quipped frankly.

"Someone has to find out what he's up to. Melinda sure ain't going to," snapped Gracie.   Libby bristled at the tone in Gracie's voice. "Could it be you just full of sour grapes, because Melinda's paying so much attention to that young man? We should be glad that she found kin folk. Look at the two of us. You haven't got anyone to call family. What have I got? One son who moved hundreds of miles away to get away from me. He seems to want to keep it that way."

"Oh surely not, Libby," said Gracie, figuring she shouldn't admit out loud that she already had thoughts along that line a long time ago.

"The only time I hear from him is when he answers a letter from me. His letters are short and to the point. Notes really. They say the same thing every time. We're fine. Hope you are too. Love Donald." Libby glared at Gracie. "I say let Melinda alone. She's happy."

Gracie gave up. She just didn't have the energy to fuss with Libby. She closed her eyes and began to gently rock.

Libby cleared her throat and asked, "Gracie, could you go in and talk to Miss Moxie. She won't let me take a book out of the library unless I pay a dollar. You really should stopped her from giving out Miss Molly's books like that."

So that's why she's hanging around me. I knew she must have a reason other than to be friendly. "Why me? I don't read as much as you do," said Gracie, rubbing the arm of her rocker.

"You the one who told her she had to get a job, besides you're better at talking to people than I am," persuaded Libby.

"You mean I'm a plain talker? I don't beat around the bush? I say just what I think?" Gracie stormed.

"Something like that," admitted Libby, looking down at her lap.

"Seems like I've heard that a lot more lately than I care to. All right, I'll give it one more try. I've been meaning to look a word up in the dictionary anyway," consented Gracie, limping on her way to the door.

Absorbed with reading, Moxie didn't notice Gracie entered the library. The older lady cleared her throat. Moxie gave her a weak smile. "Come in, Miss Gracie. How are ye doin' this fine day?"

"I wondered if I could talk to you about a couple things."

"Of course. Sure it tis, I'm not busy at the moment as ye can see. I'd be glad for the conversation. Sit down, please." Moxie motioned to the chair across the table from her. "Pray tell, what's on ye mind?"

Gracie came right to the point. "I'm worried about Melinda and this nephew of hers. You've been around him some. What do you think of him?"

"Oh, me thinks he's right easy on the eyes," cooed Moxie, dreamy look covered her face.

"Wipe that look off your face. I can see right now you're no help," snapped Gracie.

"It's sorry I am," apologized Moxie. " What did you want to know?"

"Has the man said anything about his family or where he's from to you? Don't you think he's rather closed mouthed and sneaky acting?"

"I don't think anything of the kind. I got the impression he may have had a falling out with his family some time back. It must be something that's hard for him to talk about," defended Moxie.

"Just the same, I have a bad feeling about this man. It wouldn't hurt if you were watchful of him with me for Melinda's sake."

"That I will do. I'll be glad to watch him as much as I can," Moxie said, grinning, Gracie glared at her. Moxie's face took on a serious look. "I think you're worrin' for nothin', but I will be glad to see what I can find out. Now how about checking out a book?"

"That's the other thing. Could you let Libby take books out of here like she always has? She doesn't know what to do with herself without a book in her hand. She's already been out on the porch pestering me. That's not natural for Libby. Please, tell her to keep getting books out of here for free. She'll drive me and you both crazy if you don't," pleaded Gracie.

Moxie sighed. "All right. For ye, Miss Gracie, since

Miss Libby is a resident at Moser Mansion, she can have the books without payin' the dues."

"Much obliged." Gracie walked over to the book shelves. She pretended to study the books around the open spot where Jeffrey took the book. The shelf was so high up. The print was too small for her to make out the titles.

"Are ye looking for a particular book?" asked Moxie.

Gracie pointed up. "What is the title of the book that's missing in that row?"

"Let me go through the catalog list I made. I can readily tell ye." Moxie read through a pile of papers on the table. "Here it tis. That would be, *The History Of Locked Rock And The Surrounding Rural Area.* Strange ...." Her voice trailed off as she puzzled.

"What's strange?"

Moxie looked worried. "The book hasn't been checked out. I'm the one who puts them back so they get in the right spot. It couldn't be anywhere else. I'm sorry for it being missing, if ye were wanting to check it out, Miss Gracie."

"That's all right, but didn't I tell you something would happen to some of them books if you let strangers in this library?" Gracie saw the consternation on Moxie's face and went on, "I'll get another book. Where is the dictionary? I need to look up a word."

"Oh, someone checked it out this morning," lamented Moxie. "Tis sorry I am."

"You let someone take the dictionary, too," Gracie cried in disbelief.

"For sure, I'm sorry." Moxie cried when she saw the disgruntled look on Gracie' face.

"You should be," snapped Gracie. She threw her hands up in the air in surrender.

110

Gracie intended to let Libby know she could take a book out of the Moser library any time she wanted. She opened her mouth to speak, but changed her mind, plopping back down in her rocker. Snoring like a freight train, Libby's head slanted to one side, her mouth wide open and Melinda's quilt sliding off her lap.

Jeffrey and Melinda arrived back shortly after the evening meal. The two of them burst into the parlor. Melinda, breathless from laughing at something Jeffrey said, greeted Gracie and Moxie. "We've had the greatest time. The ride was wonderful. Supper was so good. Not any better than Aunt Pearlbee's mind you but different because it was in a restaurant."

"I must confess I'm miserable. I ate way too much dinner," Jeffrey said, rubbing his stomach. He had just became aware that Gracie was staring at him. The man inhaled slowly, judging the look on her face. He managed a wide, stiff smile at her. It worked to get her to rearrange her expression. Deliberately, Gracie dropped her gaze while Jeffrey continued. "What I need is a walk around the block. Would any of you ladies care to join me?"

"Father in Heaven! No! I'm wore out," Melinda sighed as she eased herself down on the settee, rubbing her full stomach.

"I'd be glad to take a walk with you," offered Moxie.

"Wonderful, then let's go." Jeffrey offered her his arm. As they went down the hall, he was telling her about the spectacular moon rising on the eastern horizon.

"Jeffrey is such a nice man. I am so lucky we found each other," said Melinda.

"Did he tell you anything about your brother?"

"Oh yes. He has passed away and so has Jeffrey's

mother."

"Sorry to hear that," said Libby.

Gracie rubbed her toe over crest design on the rug in front of her as she thought. That wasn't what he had told her that very afternoon. She asked him about his father. She distinctly remembered his answer that he thought his father was still alive. The way he said it made her think that they just hadn't seen each other for awhile. "What did your brother look like?" asked Gracie.

"It's been such a long time. Let me see. He had sandy hair and brown eyes. A rather tall, thin man. Why do you ask?"

"I wondered if Jeffrey looked like his dad?"

Melinda thought a minute. "Not really. I suppose he takes more after his mother."

"Do you know what she looked like?"

"Sure I do. She was from Locked Rock. A pretty, young thing when they left town, but it's hard for me to remember much about her. It's been so long ago." Melinda closed her eyes and let happier days play in her mind.

It was sometime later when the silence was interrupted by the bang of the screen door.   "Listen, I believe they're back," Melinda said.

Gracie could hear Moxie's voice. "Come and let me show you the new town library, Mr. Jeffrey."

"Lead on, Miss Moxie."

Their voice grew distant except for a short laugh now and then that echoed down the hall. Time dragged by. Gracie's head nodded. She dozed off. When she woke up, she elbowed Melinda. "Wake up, sleepy head. We best hit the hay. It must be late."

"Yes, we should," Melinda said through a yawn. She frowned when she heard the distant voices in the library.

"Listen, Jeffrey hasn't left yet. Oh dear, I don't think it'd be proper to go to bed and leave the two of them alone in there."

"They've been unchaperoned for some time now while we had a cat nap. What makes the difference?"

"They didn't know that we were asleep. Surely Jeffrey will be leaving soon. Let's sit here for a while yet." Melinda looked around the room. "Libby must have went to bed."

"Reckon she did," agreed Gracie, begrudgingly. They sat in silence. Growing restless, Gracie rose from her chair. With her hands clasped behind her back, she paced around the settee. "I have half a notion to go in there and tell that young man to leave right now." She headed for the library.

"Don't do that," whispered Melinda. She jumped up to stop Gracie. Gracie halted just inside the parlor door.

Jeffrey's voice seemed closer. "Miss Moxie, would it be too presumptuous of me to want to kiss you good night?"

"No. Sure it tis, I'd say not since I've been thinking the same thing," Moxie said softly.

"Listen to that hussy," hissed Gracie.

Melinda shook her arm. "Sh! Gracie remember you were young once, too. You going to try to tell me you never let Millard Sokal kiss you? Let's get away from the door and leave them alone. Jeffrey's about to leave now."

"He just better," snapped Gracie, not wanting to dignify the rest of Melinda's question with an answer.

The ladies hurried back to their chairs and sat very still, straining to hear what was said over the beat of the grandfather clock. It struck eleven o'clock, chiming that seemed louder than usual in the stillness. Gracie gave the clock a sour look. That timepiece was trying to rub it in that they had been kept up late. Finally, she heard the soft bang of the screen door.

From that night on, Moxie took on a moony disposition

and a starry eyed look. If Gracie didn't have enough to worry about, now she had to worry about Moxie taking up with the likes of Melinda's nephew. She was pretty sure Moxie didn't intent to get friendly with that young man to find out more about him for Melinda's sake. If they only knew more about him. If he didn't act so sneaky, Gracie would feel better about him hanging around.

Next time Jeffrey showed up, he not only asked Melinda out but he invited Moxie as well. While they were gone, Gracie decided she wasn't going to spend another late night in the parlor waiting for that man to leave. She was prepared for the trio's return with a plan for turning in early that night. After all, she wasn't cut out to be a chaperon.

"Gracie, are you up?" called Melinda from down the entry hall.

"In the parlor," returned Gracie.

"We had such a good time tonight. It's so much fun being out with that young couple. Makes me feel young again." Melinda dropped down in the blue, stuffed chair next to Gracie. "Where's Libby?"

"Said she was taking a book out of the library while Miss Moxie wasn't looking and sneak it to her room to read. Speaking of the young couple, where are they?"

"They stopped off in the library to talk for awhile. I do enjoy a nice ride in the country even if it is a little cool for me," rambled Melinda. The best part is I think that Jeffrey and Miss Moxie are hitting it off just fine. They seemed to enjoy each other's company. Isn't that great, Gracie?"

"Melinda, we don't know much about your nephew unless he told you more when you've been out together. Has he?"

"Whatever he has to tell I'll hear it in time. We've been

apart for years. It's going to take time to catch up on all of his life and mine. No hurry is there?"

"Maybe not, but it seems to me he's shared very little about himself so far?"

"Oh, you're too suspicious." Melinda waved her hand weakly at Gracie.

"All I'm saying is, you should ask him for some details about your family." Gracie looked over at the grandfather clock in the corner. She got up and paced the floor by the fireplace. Tired of that, she sat back down.

"What is wrong with you? You're as nervous as a cat needing a place to potty," wondered Melinda.

"Nothing's wrong. Just never mind."

In no time, Melinda, suffering from a full stomach, doze off. The muffled voices in the library stilled. Gracie figured Jeffrey and Moxie had started to smooch. She looked at the hands on the grandfather clock. Gripping the arms of her chair, she braced herself and squeezed her eyes shut, listening to the slow tick. A long, loud, vibrating ring broke the silence, echoing down the entry hall at the same time the grandfather clock chimed ten times.

Melinda jumped. "What on earth is that noise?"

"My alarm clock in the library," admitted Gracie, watching the parlor door.

"What on earth is it doing in the library?"

"I put it there," stated Gracie, dully.

"Why?"

"That young man is going to get the message that it's time to leave at a decent hour so we can go to bed," she said matter of factly.

"Gracie! You didn't. Poor Miss Moxie. How embarrassing." Melinda hid her flushed cheeks with her hands.

115

"I did. When is he going back home anyway?" Gracie demanded.

"He hasn't said, and I'm not going to ask. I want him to stay as long as he can," cried Melinda. She headed for the door.

Gracie called after her, "My mother used to say it was time to leave when the relatives stood around in the corner of the room and whispered."

"Gracie's gone too far this time," muttered Melinda. She entered the library just as the alarm ended. Moxie rummaged through the writing table drawer, throwing all the contents on the table. "Where could that terrible racket be comin' from?"

Jeffrey, down on his knees, looked under the settee. "I don't see a thing to cause that racket under here."

"Thank goodness, the noise stopped," said Moxie.

"I'm sorry. So very sorry for this," apologized Melinda, shaking her head sideways forlornly.

"What have you got to be sorry for, Aunt Melinda?" Jeffrey asked. He stood up and brushed off his knees.

"It's not me really, but Gracie that owes you an apology. I intend to see that she gives it to you," declared Melinda, wringing her hands together.

Jeffrey put his arm around her shoulders. Aunt Melinda, you're shaking. Don't be so upset. Whatever it is Miss Gracie did, it can't be that bad?"

"You don't know. She does the most peculiar things sometimes." Melinda's lower lip quivered.

"What did she do this time?" Moxie asked, rubbing Melinda's arm.

"She hid her alarm clock in here somewhere and set it to go off at ten o'clock," whimpered Melinda.

"Horse feathers! Why would she do something like

that?" Moxie asked disbelievingly. Jeffrey grinned at her. She blushed. "Oh, me thinks I see."

"It's all right, Aunt Melinda. Really it is. I'm just leaving," assured Jeffrey.

"It's not all right at all. Gracie shouldn't be so rude. I intend to tell her so." Melinda sniffled in her hanky.

Jeffrey kissed her on the cheek. "Why don't you call it a night dear one. What is it you always say. You must be tired enough to sleep on a train track."

"I am at that." Melinda managed a weak smile and started for the door. She turned back. "You are sure you're leaving right away, Jeffrey?"

"Yes, ma'am. I'm on my way out right now," he declared.

"And I'm after escorting him out the door meself to make sure," vowed Moxie, crossing her heart.

"Very well. Good night, children," said Melinda with a yawn.

Chapter 14

Melinda left for the day with Jeffrey. Seemed like to Gracie, he kept her out longer and longer each time he came for her. Maybe it was just as well that she didn't have to face that man for very long at a time. What she thought of him had to be on her face plain as day. She hated to apologize for setting the alarm clock, but Gracie felt she had to. Melinda got so upset over such a little thing. Didn't seem like any big deal to her, but she didn't like it when Melinda stayed angry with her. Gracie just wanted things to go back the way the were between Melinda and her before this stranger showed up. She wanted Melinda sharing the porch with her again.

Gracie rubbed the back of her neck. It felt stiff from her nodding and jerking, fighting sleep. She might as well go up to her room for a nap. She started down the entry hall past the small, mahogany table that sat just inside the door. She gave the unwanted telephone a grim look. She past the library door and the parlor door. The rows of Moser family portraits, stiffly, posed people smiling grimly, stared down on her. Nora and Ned Moser's pictures were back up at the end of the line. This was a depressing hall to walk down with that row of dead people leering down at her and a panther snarling above the parasol holder over the hall table.

Something was amiss, but what was it? Gracie retraced her steps and noticed Moxie wasn't at her table in the library. She wondered for a moment where the girl could be and remembered Moxie left earlier to walk down to the post office. Gracie noticed the space in the top shelf had been filled. The book Jeffrey took was back. She wished she could read through it to see what had been so secretly interesting to Jeffrey to cause he to take it without asking. That top shelf was too high to reach without a chair. Standing on a chair really wasn't a good idea at her age. Be her luck, she'd fall and break a hip. That would cause more questions than she wanted to answer. She could go get her cane and try to jerk the book off the shelf, but her still might not be long enough reach that high. Gracie glanced around. The fainting couch would be sturdy enough to hold her up. It held up Libby the time she tromped on it when she had the fit about the cricket. She'd come back after that book when everyone went to bed.

Retracing her steps to the hall table again, she inspected the area. She still felt as if something was a miss. Next to the table was a brighter ring of boards in the middle of dusty floor. It ran through her mind if Moxie noticed how dusty that floor was, she'd have them all back at house cleaning.

It came to her what was wrong. A statue sat in that circle. The naked man plant stand had always been by that table. A three feet tall plant stand, the statue of a naked man wearing only a loin cloth. He held a large, Boston fern in a wicker pot on his head. The plant's long ruffled, light green fronds hung down to just below the statue's eyes. It always seemed to Gracie, the naked man peeked obscenely through the leaves to stare at her when she walked by. She once asked Molly to move it. Molly wouldn't do that since her mother had placed the planter in that spot after a trip to Africa. Molly wanted to leave everything in the mansion just as Nora Moser had decorated it in respect for her mother's memory. Gracie gave up on trying to change Molly's mind. The Moser estate had been the showplace of Locked Rock since 1870. Molly was proud of her home.

119

Gracie checked the library to make sure the statue hadn't been moved there. She went into the parlor and searched the room. Not there either. Gracie slumped down in her chair to think. The naked man planter definitely wasn't close by. It was too heavy for the women in the mansion to do more than scoot it into the library or parlor. It had disappeared. Someone must have stole him, but who'd want that ugly thing? Melinda's nephew maybe? Would he steal it for money? He's bound to need some money after going so long without a job. He did let Melinda pay for his meal. That's a sign he was sort of money. Not that that statue would be worth much. It'd take a strange person to want to buy that ugly thing. No offense to Nora Moser, but surely decorating tastes have changed since her day. Must be Jeffrey took it. He's up to no good. *I knew it all along.*

Gracie didn't want to hurt Melinda's feelings by accusing her nephew, but Sheriff Ben Logan should know what was going on. He might be able to find out something about Jeffrey Armstrong before he did something that they'd all regret. Perhaps she could talk the sheriff into being discreet with his investigation until he was sure that Jeffrey was a thief. She needed to send for the sheriff to explain this all to him, but who could she trust to ask that'd keep their mouth shut so Melinda or worse yet, Jeffrey wouldn't find out.

Gracie walked back out in the hall and took another look at the spot where the naked man had been for so long. She stared at the shiny circle on the floor, wondering who to ask to get the sheriff. She turned to face the telephone. Didn't Sara say the sheriff had one of those contraptions in his office? Maybe she could talk to him on that.

Gracie lifted the receiver and turned the crank.

"Hello," Sara said on the other end.

"I need to talk to the sheriff. Ring him on this here thing

for me."

"Gracie? That you? Are you all right? You sound out of breath," Sara said, concerned.

"I'm fine. Just get me the sheriff," growled Gracie.

"All right, Gracie, hold your horses."

Gracie listened to the distant, brassy bring, bring in her ear.

The familiar voice drawled, "Howdy, Sheriff Logan here. What can I do you fer?"

"Sheriff, this is Gracie Evans. I need you to come to Locked Rock quick. We had a naked man in the mansion, but I can't find him now."

"Where was he?" The sheriff asked, all business. Gracie imagined the man removing his boots from the desk and setting up straight.

"In the entry hall standing next to the little table just inside the porch door."

"But he isn't there now?"

"No, he isn't there now," bit back Gracie. Shouting at the telephone, she said, "I told you that. Can you hear good on this contraption?"

"I can hear you just fine Miss Gracie. In fact, I'm listening to you from an arm's length away if you want to know the truth. Listen, I'll never be able to make it fast enough from the county seat. I'll call Earl Bullock and send him over to help you. He just signed on as the town marshal for Locked Rock to replace Loren Stevens."

The sheriff's hung up phone clicked in her ear. Gracie started to place the receiver back in the gold hook. She put the receiver back to her hear when she heard Sara's voice. "Gracie, you still there?"

"I'm here."

121

"Get out of that house fast before that naked man turns up again," screeched Sara.

Gracie accused, "Were you listening in on me and the sheriff?"

"Just a little. I was concerned about you. Molly said for me to watch out for all of you ladies while she's gone."

"I've got everything under control so hang up now and let the sheriff call you." Gracie heard the click in her ear. She wondered how often Sara listened to the conversations of people using the telephone. Could be Sara had a new way to find out what was going on in town. Wonder if it would work for anyone who wanted to try it? No time to speculate about that nonsense now. She had a big problem to worry about.

Back up, Gracie leaned against the wall. She studied the shiny spot in the floor, trying to get a clue to what had happened to the statue. Earl's boots created hollow thuds when he ran up the porch steps brought her back to the present. She watched through the screen when he knocked on the door.

"Come on in, Earl."

The man burst in, waving a shotgun around the hall. He panted, "The sheriff said you had a naked man in here. I came as fast as I could to help. Where is the last place you saw this man?"

"He stood right here against the wall by this table. What are you waving that gun around for? There's nothing here to shoot," puzzled Gracie.

"Where did the man disappear to?"

Gracie shrugged her shoulders. "I don't know. That's why I called the sheriff."

"Miss Gracie, seeing such a horrible sight had to be a terrible shock for you, but can you describe him to me? Wait let me set this gun down and get out my note pad and pencil."

Earl licked his pencil lead. "Now how tall was he?"

"Don't take on so, Earl. I've seen that horrible sight as you called it for a long time now. I'm used to it." Gracie couldn't figure out why her neighbor was so excited.

Earl looked at her disbelievingly. "Why, Miss Gracie, ----.

"All right, to answer your question, he's three or four feet tall, I reckon."

"More like a boy then." Earl scribbled on his note pad.

Gracie paused to give that some thought. "No, from what I seen of him, he's definitely a man."

Turning red, Earl keep his eyes on his note pad and tried to keep his mind on the investigation. "Four feet is rather short for a man don't you think?"

"Well," Gracie paused to give her answer some thought. "With that fern plant on his head it made him look taller. Kind of hard to tell though."

Earl began to look dubious. He said slowly, "The naked man had a plant on his head?"

"Yip, he did."

"And you don't know which way this man went?" He tilted his head to the side, studying Gracie.

"If I knew that I wouldn't have called the law in, would I?"

"Well, I don't know," said Earl, clearly confused.

"Well, I do know. I want that naked man back before Miss Molly comes home. You going to help me like the Sheriff asked you to or not?"

Earl's forehead wrinkled with worry lines. "You want him back! Miss Gracie, it isn't like you to talk this way. Why don't you go in the parlor and sit down for a spell. I'll send Sara over to see about you."

"I'm upset. What do you expect? I don't need Sara coming over here, but you're right. I do need to sit down for awhile. This has been too much excitement for one day." Gracie rubbed her forehead.

Earl looked down at his notepad while he walked along beside Gracie, escorting her to the parlor. "Now let me see if I have the facts straight. You saw a three foot tall, naked man standing along that there wall." He turned and pointed to the spot by the table. "He took off running and disappeared, and you'd like him to come back."

"Earl Bullock, that's not what I said a tall. What kind of a lawman are you anyway? Get the sheriff down here so I can talk to him. Maybe he can get this straightened out."

"But Miss Gracie, ---."

"Just go on home and call the sheriff. Tell him I need to talk to him personally," Gracie snapped. She fell back in her chair and waved Earl away from her.

Chapter 15

Later that very afternoon, Sheriff Ben Logan rode up. He dismounted and tied his horse to the hitch rack outside the picket fence. Gracie was glad he arrived before Melinda and Jeffrey came home. She wanted to discuss the whole thing in private with the sheriff before she publicly accused Jeffrey of thievery.

As the tall, lanky lawman came through the gate, Gracie had the same old uneasy feeling creep through her that she always got when that man came near her. He still looked much like the cowboy he'd been when he worked cattle in Montana. Known as an easy talker, he could ease a confession out of any crook he came across. That sheriff was good at his job. She had to give him that.

"Howdy, Miss Gracie," Logan greeted. He slapped his cowboy hat against his jeans to shake the dust off, raising more dusty puffs from his jeans then his hat. Putting the hat back on his head, he spoke in his slow drawl, "What seems to be the trouble here? Earl was right confused about your problem."

"I'll say he was. Come up here and sit down, Sheriff, while we talk." Gracie waited until the man wedged down into the rocker beside her before she continued. "Now about Earl. He don't listen very good. Are you sure you want him to be the town marshal for Locked Rock?"

"Yes, ma'am, I'm going to give the man a try. Now tell me about the naked man you saw." With one finger, he poked the brim of his hat to raise it on his forehead.

Gracie began, "He's always standing in the hall by that

little table, and he's not there today."

"Whoa there one dad burn minute. You've seen this man more than once, and you never said anything before?"

"Sure have."

"Why didn't you say something before this?"

"Miss Molly likes him to be there. I tried to talk her into getting rid of him when I first moved in, but she wouldn't do it," Gracie responded in a matter of fact tone.

Sheriff Logan scrunched up his face while he rubbed his chin. "There's something wrong with this story, Miss Gracie. Are you sure you're feeling all right? I've known Miss Molly for years. She'd never allow no naked man to stand around in her hallway."

"I'm telling you she did just that. Now he's gone, and I want him back before Miss Molly gets back from her honeymoon."

"Why on earth would you want him back?"

Gracie wished the sheriff would quit looking at her like she had gone senile. "Don't ask me that cause I cain't tell you. It's Miss Molly that likes him."

The sheriff slowly shook his head, trying a different line of questioning. "Well, which way did he run the last time you saw him?"

"He cain't run," answered Gracie, flatly.

"He can't."

"No! For goodness sakes, the thing is an ugly old statue. He's not alive. Sheriff, haven't you been listening to me a tall? I swear you and Earl Bullock make a good pair. Heaven help us law biding citizens." Gracie stopped to take a deep breath than said very slowly, "Let me make this as plain as I can. Someone stole Miss Molly's naked man statue."

"A statue!" Trying very hard not to grin through the

serious look on his face, the sheriff said, "Someone stole a statue from Miss Molly. Is that what you've been telling me?"

Gracie slapped the rocker arm. "Finally, now you have it, Sheriff."

"When did it happen?"

"Cain't say for sure. Never liked looking at him so Miss Molly said I should look the other direction when I walked by him. That's what I did so I don't know when he disappeared."

"Seen any strangers around lately?"

"Sure lots of people I didn't know came to the wedding. Cain't say for sure who would take something of Miss Molly's, but most of the strangers here were her kin folks. I do have a suspicion that Melinda's nephew that just showed up might be the one who would take things. I been meaning to ask you to check him out and see if you can find out anything about his background. He seems sneaky to me."

The sheriff said curtly, "All right give me the details, and I'll get right on it."

"His name is Jeffrey Armstrong. He says he's from a small town called Montevallo, Missouri, but he talks like a city slicker and calls dinner lunch and supper dinner."

The sheriff shrugged his shoulders. "What's wrong with that, Miss Gracie?"

"It's just not what a man from the south that was brought up on a farm would say. That's is what's wrong with it. The man doesn't have a southern accent. He changes the subject when I try to ask him things. He always acts like he's checking out everything around him or expecting to see someone he doesn't want to see."

"So far don't seem to me to be much wrong with any of that ma'am."

"Take my word for it. That man doesn't come from a

southern state like he says. Besides he lied to me or Melinda one. I asked him about his father. Jeffrey told me his father was alive as far as he knew. A few hours later, Melinda asked about her brother, Jeffrey's father. He told her the man was dead. I saw him with my own eyes take a book off one of the library shelves and hide it under his suit coat the day of Miss Molly's wedding."

"He stole a book?" Sheriff Logan leaned forward, beginning to show some interest.

"Well … not exactly stole it," Gracie hesitated. The sheriff shot her a exasperated look. "He did bring it back."

"The man didn't steal it then, did he?" Sheriff Logan losing his patience.

"No, it was just the sneaky way Jeffrey took the book in the first place that bothered me," Gracie defended herself.

"All right, Miss Gracie, I'll look into his background. First off, I'll see if I can find out whether he lived in Missouri and go from there. Doesn't sound like I have much to go on."

"Do me a big favor though and don't say anything about this around Melinda until we know something for sure. She's real taken by Jeffrey. She wouldn't like it if she knew I had you checking him out."

Sheriff Logan nodded. "Sure thing, Miss Gracie. I'll not say anything to anyone but you if I find out something about the man."

"Thanks Sheriff and be on the lookout for the naked man. Will you? I don't know how we're going to explain him being gone to Miss Molly. She sets great store by that statue."

"Yes ma'am. I'll do my best to track the naked man down. Now I best go explain this to Earl so he can help me," said the sheriff, struggling to get out of the rocker.

Gracie advised, "Go slow when you talk to him. Maybe

he'll catch on quicker this time."

"I'll do that," agreed the sheriff. Touching his hat brim, he grinned at her.

That evening, Gracie stretched out on her bed and waited for movements in the other bedrooms to stop. Finally, she slipped off the bed. Easy as she could, she opened her door and peeked out in the hall. With her ear turned to the empty hall, she listened a moment and decided it was safe to walk out into the hall. It made her nervous how loud the creaks of the floor boards sounded when she stepped on them, but she kept to her sure, hushed course. The mansion was darker than dark. Gracie had to feel her way down the stairs and along the entry hall, taking baby steps for fear she'd fall.

She breathed easier after she shut the library door behind her. Making her way over to the writing table, she opened the small drawer and felt for a match to light the lamp. The library sprang into soft reality with shadows in the far corners. The colorful book bindings glowed like they were on fire where the lamplight touched them. Without hesitation, Gracie made her way to the end section and gazed up at the top shelf. The book was still there.

She grunted when she picked up on the end of the fainting couch to swivel it around in front of the shelves. She hadn't realized it'd be so heavy. She was glad when she had it at the base of the shelves. She crawled onto it and over to the shelves. Using them for a handhold, Gracie very slowly stood up. At first, she wasn't sure she'd be able to reach the book yet. Standing on tiptoes, she leaned against the shelves and stretched as far as she could. With the tips of her fingers under the bottom of the book, she pulled it toward her. The book teetered on the edge of the shelf and came tumbling down, glancing off Gracie's shoulder before it hit the floor. The noise shattered the silence. Gracie leaned against the book shelves, froze to the spot. She listened for the house full of people to erupt. She breathed a sigh of relief when she didn't hear running footsteps. She dropped to her knees and crawled to the edge of the fainting couch. Swinging her legs around, she stood up on the floor. Gracie grabbed the end of the couch and scooted it against the wall where it had been. Excitement tingled in her when she picked up the book. She blew the lamp out and edged her way to the door. Putting her ear to the door, she listened for sounds. For a second, she froze, thinking she heard someone breathing until she realized it was her own. Slowly, she turned the knob and winced when it clicked softly. Cracking the door, she peeked out. The coast was clear. Holding the book close, she hugged the dark, hallway wall and made her way back to her room.

Late into the night, Gracie read the book. When she finished the last page, she gave up the puzzle with a regretful sigh. None of the information leaped out at her from those pages. Now she had to put the book back where she found it without getting caught. Prowling around the house late at night in the dark hadn't been fun. She shook her head, feeling thick headed tiredness. Morning would be dawning all too soon. Time to sleep. She'd worry about what to do with the book in the morning.

Chapter 16

Gracie opened the front screen door with one hand and squeezed her quilt under her arm and against her with the other hand. "Lady bugs are back," she mumbled. She swiped at the tiny, red insects sunning in her rocker seat. A couple of them moved slowly along the arm of the rocker as if traveling was an effort. They spread their wings to fly a short distances before they lit again.

Gracie would like to brought the insect invasion to someone's attention, but there wasn't anyone around to tell the news that would care. In the library, Moxie waited for customers. Libby, reading in the parlor, would have a spell rather than come close to a bug which might happen anyway when some of the little critters decided to come indoors. What Gracie really wanted to do was tell Melinda. She was the one Gracie shared things like this with. They use enjoy talking about such things, but Melinda wasn't here. She was out for another one of those ride with Jeffrey. Shopping they said.

Two lady bugs crawled over the rocker arm right next to Gracie's arm. Gracie watched the insects flap their wings in an effort to lift off, but they failed. She helped them along by flipping them one at a time with her fingers. Before she had time to think about it, three lady bugs took over the rocker arm.

While she occupied herself by flicking the insects off onto the porch floor, Gracie's thoughts turned to what she succeeded at doing that morning. She smiled at how she managed to returned the book without getting caught. Every morning, Moxie left the library unattended when she went to the post office. Rocking, Gracie watched for Moxie to leave. She walked into the empty library, brought the book out from under her shawl and left it on top the stack on the table.

Gracie watched Moxie return with a handful of mail. She closed her eyes and pretended to be napping. In a few minutes, running footsteps sounded in the hall. The screen door squeaked open and slammed shut, bounced and vibrated closed.

Gracie flinched and turned to see Moxie steaming down on her. "What's all the racket about?"

"Tis sorry I am if I woke you up, Miss Gracie. I thought you'd want to know I just found that missing copy of *The History Of Locked Rock*. It was on the very top of the returned books I have to put back on the shelves," Moxie said, mystified. "Who brought it back while I was gone?"

Gracie said innocently, "I didn't noticed anybody come to visit while you were gone. As you can plainly see, I was taking a nap which you like to scared me to death waking me up from. Could be someone slipped by me."

"It did return no worse for wear," Moxie decided. "I should be grateful."

Gracie couldn't help herself. She had to get a dig in about the ill fated library. "I warned you what would happen when you cain't keep good track of Miss Molly's books. You just lucked out this time."

Moxie didn't say another word, but she did look rather huffy when she went back inside.

"What you doing, Gracie?"

Gracie flinched. She had been so absorbed in flipping the lady bugs she failed to notice she had company. Sara Bullock stood at the base of the steps. Gracie wondered how she managed to let Sara slip up that close. *Be my luck, I'm getting hard of hearing, too.* "What you want, Sara?" She grumped.

"Can I sit with you for a spell?" asked Sara, timidly.

"Reckon so. Shouldn't you be watching that switchboard?" grumbled Gracie.

"Earl is spelling me so I can have a break. That's allowed," said Sara, defending herself.

Gracie straightened up in her rocker and squared her shoulders. "Oh? How does Earl have time to do that? Shouldn't he be out policing the town?"

"Gracie, what has you in such a foul mood?" Sara sat down in the rocker next to the elderly lady.

"Didn't know I was?"

"Take it from me you are," confirmed Sara.

"Sorry about that. Reckon I have a lot on my mind," Gracie said softly, looking away from Sara.

"Maybe I can cheer you up. I thought by now the Moser mansion ladies must be missing Molly something awful. Maybe you'd like a change of scene and something different to do so I wondered if you'd all like to come to my house tomorrow night for supper. It's Earl's birthday. We'd like to have you ladies help him celebrate it. While we're at it, we're going to have a Halloween party at the same time. How about it?" Sara gave Gracie smile, hoping to lighten her mood.

"I don't know. I'm not much for parties. Best check it out with the others first before you start cooking," grumped Gracie.

"All right. Where is everyone?" Asked Sara, looking disappointed.

"Miss Moxie's in the library where she is everyday. Libby is in the parlor. Who knows where Melinda is. She's off gallivanting around with that man that says he's her nephew,"

133

groused Gracie.

Sara gave Gracie a hard look and repeated Gracie's words. "That says he's her nephew. Don't you believe him?"

"Nope."

"Why on earth not?"

"He says things that don't seem right," Gracie answered shortly.

Sara studied Gracie a second. She looked confident she had hit on what was causing Gracie's sour mood. "I see. It couldn't be that you're missing Melinda's company. Maybe a little jealous of all the time she's spending with her new found relative."

Gracie straightened in her chair and faced Sara. "Libby said the same thing. That's not it at all. I just have the feeling that something isn't right about that young man. He's .... sneaky."

"Have you talked to Melinda about this?" Sara asked, raising her eyebrows in an expressive manner.

"I've tried to, but it didn't do me any good. She's blinded by his slick ways," Gracie said, seriously.

"You better go slow about your suspicions until you have some proof. You'd hurt Melinda if you're wrong. Wouldn't be right to accuse her nephew falsely," cautioned Sara

"I know that. I don't care a hoot what that young man thinks, but Melinda wouldn't ever speak to me again. That's what worries me. I just wish someone would see that man like I see him," confirmed Gracie.

Late Halloween afternoon, Gracie and Melinda waited in the parlor for Libby and Moxie to join them. The other residents eagerly accepted Sara's invitation and talked Gracie into going.

"What's that nephew of yours doing tonight? He's usually here by now," inquired Gracie, looking for conversation.

"I told him I had to go to Sara's for supper. I invited him to go with us, but he said he might have something else to do tonight."

"Wonder what that'd be? He hasn't done anything else but come here since he's been in town. Seems awful closed mouthed to me, and he don't seem to be getting much better. Has he said much more about his life?" Gracie pried.

"Oh, he talks about it if I ask him, but I don't want to appear nosy," Melinda answered half heartedly.

"Maybe being nosy wouldn't hurt just to be sure he's on the up and up," suggested Gracie.

"Father in Heaven!" Melinda cried, rolling her eyes dramatically toward the ceiling. "Don't start that again. Why wouldn't Jeffrey be telling me the truth. What would he have to gain by lying about being related to me."

"Maybe he thinks you have some money he could inherit later or borrow now."

"If he did, he surely has changed his mind by now. He can tell how I live. No, I choose to believe him, and I hope he stays around awhile," Melinda snapped, defending her nephew.

Gracie held her hands palm up toward Melinda. "All right. If you say so." She had to give Melinda credit. She had the backbone to stick up for something when she thought she was right.

"Hello, anyone home," came Jeffrey's voice from the front door.

Melinda clapped her hands together. "Wonderful, he did decide to join us. Miss Moxie will be tickled, I'll bet," she said, winking at Gracie.

135

"He's probably more interested in a free meal," groused Grace under her breath.

Melinda frowned, but she didn't have time to do more than back hand Gracie on the shoulder before Jeffrey entered. Rubbing her shoulder, Gracie stood up and walked past him, in no mood to greet him. She walked through the dining room to the foot of the stairs and yelled, "Miss Moxie, Libby, hurry up. It's time to go. We'll be late for supper."

"I'm ready, Miss Gracie," Moxie replied. She started down the stairs followed by Libby.

Gracie noted that Moxie's new dress, a white dress covered with little blue circles. Black lace trimmed the bodice and a couple rows edged the high collar and on the cuffs.

With Gracie in the lead, the three ladies trouped into the parlor. Moxie brightened when she saw Jeffrey waiting for her. "Well, hello." She greeted with a smile.

Gracie edged close to Melinda and whispered in her ear. "Look at that young woman all decked out in a new dress. I'd say that girl knew more about your nephew coming to visit then you did."

With a finger tapping her lips, Melinda gave Gracie a slight grin.

When Earl opened the door, all sorts of good food smells blasted the women. Each expressed their birthday wishes to him as they scattered out and sat down in the front room. In no time, Sara came to the door to invite them into the kitchen. she seated them around the table. Earl said grace before Sara started passing bowls of mash potatoes, gravy, baked duck and stuffing, and a relish plate of late veggies from the garden.

Finishing up the last bite on his plate, Earl dropped his fork with a clatter. He rubbed his stomach. "Mighty good food, wife."

"Thank you, birthday boy," Sara said, smiling at her husband.

"Jeffrey how about you and me go to the front room and get comfortable while the women clean up the kitchen before they ask us to help do dishes," Earl said, chuckling.

"Sounds like a plan to me," Jeffrey said, winking at Moxie. As he rose from the table, he said, "Thank you for the delicious meal, Mrs. Bullock."

"You're quite welcome, Mr. Armstrong," Sara replied warmly.

Later, the women joined the Earl and Jeffrey. They just sat down when the switchboard rung.

"Reckon I best go answer that," Sara groaned. She eased off the couch, hating to move.   Everyone looked at Sara questioningly when she returned. Gracie asked, "Who was it?"

"Doctor's needed out at the Swinson farm right quick. Mrs. Swinson is having her baby. Her husband says she's been at it all day. Lucky for her, he was home when I rang him," Sara replied, looking worried.

"Tis miserable she looked a few days ago when she came to the library to check out a book. For sure, it's good for her that her time is up," said Moxie.

"It's their first, isn't it?" asked Melinda.

"That's right," answered Sara. "Let's hope everything goes all right. First time labor isn't always a fast moving event."

"Sure and me thinks, it might be even worse tonight. It's a bad night to be having a baby what with it being Halloween," determined Moxie.

"Why?" asked Gracie.

"Babes born on Halloween are said to have special powers come on them," warned Moxie. "That's not always a good thing."

"Like what?" inquired Melinda.

"The wee ones grow up with the ability to perceive and talk to those that have gone on before us," explained Moxie in a know it all tone.

"Where did you get a crazy notion like that?" spit out Gracie.

"My dada told me. He used to tell us stories he brought over from Ireland. That's not all. He told stories of spirits that roamed the earth on Halloween and witches who worshiped the devil," said Moxie in a hushed voice.

"My birthday is tonight," suggested Earl. The corners of his mouth twitched.

"Can you talk to the dead?" scoffed Gracie.

"Haven't bothered to try, Miss Gracie." Earl looked at Moxie. She watched his reaction intently to see if he was taking her seriously. "But that don't mean I won't some day." He grinned at Moxie and winked. Then he went back to puffing on his pipe.

She grinned back. Earl going along with her gave her the confidence to continue. "Dada used to tell us about how the Jack O' Lantern started, too. There once was a man named Jack in Ireland who died on Halloween. He couldn't enter Heaven, because he had been a miser that didn't tithe. The devil didn't want Jack, because he had played a trick on him. So Jack has been forced to walk the earth swinging his Jack O' Lantern on Halloween until Judgment day. Folks felt sorry for him and put their own jack o'lantern out on Halloween night to help light Jack's way."

"Sure," snorted Gracie.

"I don't know about that Jack feller, but some folks do believe that folks who don't rest easy when they die will be back about this time of year or even oftener," offered Earl.

"Really?" exclaimed Libby from the rocker next to the window. She had a nervous look on her face.

Earl took his pipe out of his mouth and began, "Just last night I met up with Jake Myers over in the saloon. He looked plum shook. Told me he had been out all day shoeing horses south of town down past the illy pond by the colonies. He started back for Locked Rock just at dusk. That's where he liked to got the pants scared offen him. You ought to know that pond, Miss Gracie. Your farm and Orie's aren't too far from it."

"I remember it all right. Full of white flowers come June and big leafed lilies the rest of the time. If there was to be a fish in that water, there'd be no way to get a hook in to catch it," declared Gracie.

"Well for goodness sakes, go on with your story, Earl. What happened to Jake?" asked Sara, impatiently.

"Jake said a young woman stepped out of the underbrush onto the road right in front of his mount. Spooked the horse. He reared up. Jake had all he could do to hang on. By the time he got that horse settled down, he looked up and down the road. The woman had just flat out disappeared."

"Who was she?" asked Gracie.

Earl continued, "He said he'd never met her before, but there was something peculiar about her. She was a thin, sickly looking woman. She was sobbing and holding her arms out toward him. She acted like she needed help, but he couldn't find hide nor hair of her near the road so he came on home. Decided to get him a drink. He was that shook up. He couldn't figure how that woman could disappear in thin air so fast."

139

Sara shook her finger in the air. "Say, Gracie, wasn't there something years ago about a neighbor of yours. A young woman named Rozella Thorne that had some trouble. She lived near that Lilly pond," remembered Sara.

"I heard all sorts of tales," replied Gracie.

"Tell us what happened to Rozella, Miss Gracie," suggested Moxie.

Gracie shook her head. "I was too young to get the straight of it. Earl, do you know what happened?"

Earl leaned back, got comfortable and took a puff on his pipe before he began, "Sure do. Rozella died young. Her pa wouldn't let her marry the man who asked her. He said she could do better than that fellow. Seems she was in a family way and feared her pa so much, she was afraid to tell him that or go again his wishes. She walked off in the lily pond one night to do herself in. Neighbors heard her screams for help from miles around. They figured Rozella might have changed her mind about dying, but couldn't get untangled from the lilies to save herself. By the time folks arrived to help her, Rozella had gone under. Her body never did surface. When her suitor heard about Rozella, he went off in the timber and shot himself dead. After that, folks saw Rozella roaming the road along the lily pond. She was crying for her lost love.

Pa liked to rehash that story on Halloween every year to scare the daylights out of us younguns. He'd tell how Rozella came out of no where onto the road in front of passerbys and held her arms out to them, crying her eyes out. Back then I thought he just wanted to scare us into staying home so we wouldn't pull pranks on any of the neighbors. Later on I heard others tell of seeing that woman after dark in that very spot. I'd think back to what Pa told us."

"Why do you suppose she pick Halloween to come

back?" asked Melinda

"It was her birthday," said Earl softly. "Say, Sara, you may have something here. It might have been Rozella Thorne that Jake Myers saw. I'll have to remind him about her when I see him again."

Libby frowned out the window at the darkness. "If anyone has a reason to rest uneasy, it'd be poor Rachel Simpson that was murdered next door. Reckon she might show up tonight?"

"Just never know, Miss Libby." Earl stopped talking and puffed on his pipe. He studied the smoke clouds above his head. Breaking the silence around him, he repeated softly, "You never know," he repeated softly.

Melinda tried to absorbed the concept. "Earl, do you suppose that people come back looking exactly the way they did when they died?"

"Reckon they do. Least wise they ain't never gonna age if it were a young person."

"No, I don't mean aging. Do you suppose Rachel Simpson would come back looking all bloody and with her throat cut? That she could just step out of the darkness looking the way she looked when she died?" Melinda's voice trailed off. She squeezed her eyes shut at the horrible thought.

Earl grimaced. "I reckon they do."

The room was so quiet, the only sound was the squeak of Libby rocking.

"Land sakes, let's change the subject before we scare each other to death," laughed Sara. She laughed nervously. "I have a game for us to play."

"Games are for kids," scoffed Gracie.

"I think you might like this one. Wait a minute while I go to the kitchen." Sara disappeared. She returned, carrying a

141

tray of cups and a pot of coffee.

"What kind of game is this?" grumped Libby.

"Just wait a minute. This isn't the game. Give me a minute." Sara left again. She came back with a tray of little cakes. "I didn't make Earl a birthday cake this year. I decided to make these instead."

Moxie exclaimed, "Will ye just look! Each wee cake is iced with the outline of a jack o' lantern drawn in black in the middle. What fun."

"Let me tell you about the game. It's called a fortune telling game. There's a prize baked in each of these cakes so bite easy. I'd hate it if one of you break a tooth. If you find a penny that means you'll become rich, if you find a thimble that means you'll never marry and if you find a ring you'll soon be getting married. Now pick a cake." She walked along in front of the guests, holding the tray down.

Jeffrey bit into his and came up with a penny right away. "I'll find a fortune." He smiled at Melinda like he hoped that wish would come true. Gracie hoped there wasn't thoughts going through his head of that woman being his means to the fortune.

Gracie pulled a thimble off her lip with the crumbs. "Humph, it don't take much fortune telling to know I'm not going to get married at this late date."

Melinda held up a crumb covered penny. She giggled. "Well my fortune has already come true. As far as I'm concerned since Jeffrey showed up I've been rich."

Moxie bit into her cake. She pulled a gold ring out of her mouth. Blushing, she looked at Jeffrey. He grinned at her. She lowered her head, bashfully blushing.

Libby kept eating.

"Libby, what did you get?" Sara asked.

142

"Haven't found anything, but the cake is good," she said with a full mouth. "Oh no!" she groaned, grabbing her throat. Giving a loud gulp, Libby gagged then coughed. She gasped for air, turning red faced. Finally, she stammered, "I swallowed whatever was in the cake. I hope it doesn't make me sick."

"Don't worry, Libby," said Gracie, winking at the very upset Sara. "That too shall pass."

"You can be calm. You aren't the one who has something metal going into your stomach. I don't feel good. I need to go home and go to bed, but I don't want to walk across the street alone," whined Libby.

"It's getting late. Libby's right. She needs to lay down now. Perhaps, we all should think about calling it a night," suggested Melinda, looking sorry for Libby.

"I'll be glad to escort you ladies home," offered Jeffrey.

Walking across the dark street, Melinda muttered, "It's sure spooky out here tonight." She darted a glance behind her and to the sides then edged closer to Gracie.

"You're just nerved up from listening to those silly ghost stories," scoffed Gracie. "Relax, Halloween will be over in a couple of hours. All the spooks will leave for where ever they stay until next year." She grinned when Moxie and Libby edged closer to Jeffrey.

A new moon raced madly through the tatters of black clouds. Patches of moonlight silvered everything. Growing shadows loomed out from the trees and bushes, fueled by the moon. A dog howled, sending chills up Gracie's spine. Even she admitted she'd be glad when the short walk home was over.

Chapter 17

In the middle of the night, something shattered downstairs. Gracie sat straight up in bed, listening to the creaks and groans of the old house. She tried to decipher what woke her up. After a period of quiet, she decided she was mistaken about the direction of the noise. Maybe something happened out in the street.

Suddenly, she thought about the missing statue. Maybe the thief had come back to steal again. She ought to take a look around downstairs. She lit the kerosene lamp beside her bed and grabbed her father's sassafras cane propped against the wall beside the bed. She had come to rely on that cane more and more when her knee gave out. This time, she held it like a weapon.

Gliding as quietly as she could down the hall to Melinda's room, Gracie opened her door and whispered, "Wake up, Melinda."

"What's wrong out there? I heard a noise," she whimpered.

Gracie replied in a lowered voice, "I think there's someone downstairs prowling around. Maybe trying to steal something."

"What are we going to do?" Melinda squeaked.

"I got my pa's cane. I'm going to go find out what's going on. Come with me."

"I'll go with you, but we better take Miss Moxie and Libby with us," whispered Melinda, holding her chest.

"Libby's a bad idea. If we tell her someone's sneaking

around downstairs, she'd only go into hysterics. She never be able to get out of bed and make enough noise to scare off whoever it is before we get there. I'm not sure Moxie would be any good, either. She is an accident waiting to happen if you ask me," stated Gracie, bluntly.

"Gracie, there's safety in numbers. Miss Moxie is younger than us. We better take her along, or I won't go," hissed Melinda, tugging her nightcap down over her curls.

"All right, but it's against my better judgment, but let's get going before the thief steals Miss Molly blind," urged Gracie.

They hustled down the hall. Gracie opened Moxie's door. "Miss Moxie, wake up."

Moxie's sleep thickened voice asked, "What's the matter?"

"Sh!" Both of the older ladies said together as they rushed over to Moxie's bed.

"What's the matter?" Moxie whispered, quickly sitting up. She rubbed her eyes.

"There's someone downstairs," hissed Gracie, sitting her lamp down on the bedside table.

"Are ye sure? Ye might be imagining things or having a bad dream. With all those spooky stories Earl and I told tonight, it makes for an uneasy sleep. Truly, tis sorry I am if I caused you an uneasy sleep," apologized Moxie.

"No, I didn't imagine that noise. Are you coming with us or not?" growled Gracie in a low tone.

"All right, I'll come. I told Molly I'd look after the two of ye so I better humor ye," Moxie said patronizingly. She struggled into her robe.

"Well, we're much obliged for that, but hurry up will you before the thief gets away," hissed Gracie.

"Let's take the lamp." Moxie reached for the kerosene lamp.

"Are you crazy?" Gracie pushed her hand away.

"Why not take it?" Snapped Melinda

"We'd be sitting ducks if someone's down there. We want to sneak up on whoever it is and not have him sneak up on us," reasoned Gracie.

Melinda sucked in a breath and grabbed Gracie by the shoulder. "Suppose it's Rachel Simpson haunting our house."

"Stop talking that way," scolded Gracie. "You're not helping yourself with thoughts like that. Calm down."

"It's all right, Miss Melinda," consoled Moxie. She put her arm around the older lady's waist. "Surely it's too late for a spirit now. We've been in bed awhile. The time has to be after midnight by now. Halloween tis over."

"Oh, good," breathed Melinda. "Let's go then."

The women edged along the dark hall. They started down the stairs one step at a time, stopping to listen often. The dining room was empty. Gracie slipped over to the kitchen door. She cocked an ear to the door then peeked in. No one in there.

"Miss Moxie, slip out the back door and go after Uncle Malachi," ordered Gracie.

"I don't think I should leave ye two here alone," worried Moxie.

"Go on. We might need a man's help. We'll be all right until you get back, "assured Gracie, giving the young woman a push into the kitchen.

Moxie turned back. "Miss Molly would have my head if I let one of ye get hurt. Promise me to stay right here then until I return," begged Moxie.

"Promise," grunted Gracie. "Now go."

146

As soon as Moxie slipped out the back door, Gracie turned to Melinda. "Let's check out the parlor and the library."

"You just promised Miss Moxie you'd stay right here. I heard you," complained Melinda.

"No, I never. All I did was say the word promise. I didn't say what I promised," replied Gracie.

Raising her cane up in the air, she tugged on the reluctant Melinda to get her started down the hall. Gracie stepped into the still parlor. Melinda's loud, rapid breaths came from behind her. She squinted, trying make out if there was anything usual about the room.

Suddenly a dark form, the shape of a man's head, appeared above the settee. Melinda squealed. Gracie yelled, "There he is, hiding behind the settee. Let's get him." She raised her cane high in the air with both hands and charged the settee. The head disappeared. Next came the pat of palms and thuds of knees as the man crawled across the floor.

Gracie peered over the settee. The man's head peeked from behind her chair. "There he is behind my chair." She rounded the settee.

The man ducked back behind the chair. "Wait, Miss Gracie. Don't hit me."

"Father in Heaven, it's Jeffrey. Don't hurt him, Gracie," pleaded Melinda. Rushing up behind Gracie, she grabbed her arms to lower the cane.

"What are you doing in here this time of night?" She shook Melinda's hand off and kept her cane poised in the air, inching toward her chair.

"I was sleeping on the settee." Jeffrey said meekly, peering over the chair.

"Jeffrey, why aren't you in your room at the hotel?" questioned Melinda. For the first time, Gracie heard a hint of

147

doubt creep into Melinda's voice.

"I'm so sorry, Aunt Melinda. I had to give up my room. I am temporarily out of funds, you see," he admitted sheepishly, standing up behind the chair.

Footsteps tromped in the hall. The parlor lit up. Libby burst into the room, carrying a lamp. "What is all the shouting about?"

"Jeffrey was down here in the dark. Made a noise that liked to scared us to death," accused Gracie. She kept her cane pointed at him.

Jeffrey combed his fingers through his unruly hair. "I'm dreadfully sorry to have waken you, ladies." He pointed to pile of shattered blue glass with the fringed lamp shade resting in the middle of it. "I bumped the table lamp over in the dark, feeling my way around to the front of the settee. Indeed, I am very sorry, but I couldn't pay for my room any longer. I didn't have any place else to sleep. I thought I could sneak in and back out of here in the morning before you woke up just like I've been doing."

"Whoa! You've slept down here before. How long have you been doing that?" demanded Gracie, bracing her feet to do battle.

Jeffrey rubbed his forehead. "This is the third night. I've upset all of you. I'm so very sorry for that. I'll leave now," he said forlornly.

"Just one moment. We have a spare bedroom. You can use it until you get back on your feet," offered Melinda, rushing to her nephew's side to stop him.

"That's not a good idea. What will people say about all of us single women living here with a man," snapped Libby.

"Miss Libby's right. It's not proper," agreed Jeffrey.

"Oh, and sneaking in here to sleep after we've gone to

bed is proper?" Gracie snorted.

Melinda put her hand on Jeffrey's arm. She declared firmly, "Stop this nonsense, all of you. We have a bedroom you can use, Jeffrey, and you're not a stranger. You're my nephew so I say you should be able to stay here." She glared at Libby and Gracie, defying them to argue with her.

More footsteps sounded in the hallway. "They must be in the parlor, Uncle Malachi. I see a light in there," panted Moxie. "Saint Preserve us, what's happened here?" she asked, walking around the mess at the end of the settee.

Malachi saw Gracie had her cane pointed at Melinda's nephew. He edged over close to Gracie. "Mr. Jeffrey, whats ya all doing here this time a night?" He asked.

"Mr. Jeffrey snuck in here to sleep on the settee, because he couldn't pay for a room at the hotel. He broke the lamp in the dark," Gracie answered Malachi for him..

"Melinda told him he could stay in the spare bedroom. I don't think that's a good idea, Miss Moxie," grumped Libby, shaking her head reproachfully.

Moxie glanced from Gracie fiddling with her cane to the defiant Melinda, defending her nephew. Her eyes met Jeffrey's hopeful look, and she melted. "Sure and it tis, I see no reason he can't stay in the spare bedroom. Molly wouldn't mind a relative of one of us spending some time in the mansion while they're visiting. I think it'd be all right," decided Moxie.

"Thank you so much. You'll go to Heaven in a sugar bowl for being so kind to Jeffrey," praised Melinda.

"Indeed she will. Thank you for helping me, dear lady. Now if you'll be so kind to show me the way to my room, I suggest we all turn in for the night. It is rather late, and I've caused you to miss enough sleep tonight." Jeffrey yawned, trying to cement the point.

As soon as the other ladies walked out of the parlor Gracie closed in on Jeffrey and whispered, "Our talk isn't over yet. I'm not through with you."

Jeffrey grated through clinched teeth, "I didn't suppose you was, ma'am." He turned to leave. Swirling with the swiftness Gracie hadn't expected he closed the distance between them and grabbed her arm. His fingers felt unpleasantly hot like he was about by her. Angrily, he continued in a low voice for only her ears, "But for Aunt Melinda's sake and maybe your own, you should leave well enough alone. Remember that old saying, "Curiosity killed the cat". The arrogant man's piercing, blue eyes turned icy.

The young man and Gracie stood staring at each other for a long, challenging moment. Neither of them wanted to give in to looking away. Jeffrey was putting a scare into Gracie, but she didn't want him to realize that. She was ready to put some distance between them, but she didn't now how.

"Coming Jeffrey?" Melinda's distant voice called from down the hall.

"Right behind you, Aunt Melinda," he answered warmly. He lowered his hand and walked away Gracie out the door.

Shaken by his words and angry manner, Gracie couldn't move. She tried to calm the fear that welled up in her. She glanced around the dark parlor. It might not be a good thing to stay in that room alone. She ventured after the others. Feeling a certain dread at what could happen next, she was even more convinced this strange man who professed to being Melinda's nephew was hot tempered to the point of being capable of violence. Now he wasn't just visiting, but living with them.

Chapter 18

The first of November the weather took a turned for the worse. A snow storm floated down one morning, coating the porch and ground white. By later that afternoon, Gracie stuck her head out the door to check the storm. Piles of snow covered the rockers.

She settled down again in her chair to stare at the fire in the parlor fireplace. Someone tapped on the front door. Gracie waited to see if anyone else would pass by the parlor door on the way to answer the door. No one did. It was up to her to see who was there. She limped back down the hall. Before she could reach the door, the knocking grew insistent and louder.

Gracie opened the door. Standing ankle deep in snow, three girls and two boys, with blotchy pink faces, looked expectantly at her. "What do you want?"

"To -- to come inside. You're a snow home," stuttered the tallest girl timidly between chattering teeth..

"What are you talking about?" Gracie asked, standing her ground in the door.

"The teacher said come here until we could go home," explained a red haired boy. His face was plastered with freckles that stood out starkly against his cold skin.

"That teacher was wrong. Go somewhere else." Gracie slammed the door shut. She twirled around to lean against it to keep the children out. She found herself face to face with Moxie and Melinda.

"Who's at the door on a day like this?"

"A bunch of kids that wanted to come in. I told them to go on home," said Gracie.

151

With concern for the children, Moxie reasoned, "To be sure, don't ye remember Molly said this is a snow home."

Gracie nodded slowly. "I remember all right. I'm the one that said I didn't like it."

"Gracie, that's not nice," scolded Melinda. She shoved Gracie out of the way and opened the door. The children had waded through the knee deep snow down the steps. "Come back, children. Mercy! Look out there, Gracie. You can't even see Earl and Sara's house across the street."

"It wouldn't be right to turn the wee ones away now, would it? Let's go in by the fire and warm up, children," said Moxie, leading them to the parlor door. "I'll get Aunt Pearlbee to fix some hot cocoa. You two get them out of those wet coats and shoes."

"Let them go somewhere else. They'll be nothing but trouble," grumbled Gracie to know one in particular. She avoided stepping in the clumps of snow quickly melting into little pools on the hall floor.

Melinda turned at the parlor door. Shaking her finger at Gracie, she chastised in a low voice, "Gracie, you saw what the weather was like. It's not safe for anyone outside right now, especially children. Besides Miss Molly told their teacher they could come here."

"That was if she was here. I never heard her say we had to keep them if she wasn't here. Let's use that telephone to call her and settle this," complained Gracie.

"We aren't going to do any such thing. She's on her honeymoon. We aren't going to bother her. The children are staying right here, and that's final," declared Melinda, helping the littlest girl out of her coat.

Libby looked up from a book. She gave the children a scathing once over like they were insects. "Where are we going to put them all?" She worried.

Libby looked like she might be on Gracie's side for once. Edging away from the children toward her, Gracie suggested in a lowered voice, "Help me herd them up to Miss Molly's room and lock them in."

Melinda rushed over to stand between Libby and Gracie. She whispered, "We can't do that."

"This was Miss Molly's idea. She ain't here. Let them tear up her room," declared Gracie, keeping her eyes on the children to make sure they didn't turn destructive.

"Gracie, some of the children are boys and some are girls?" Melinda pointed out.

"So what?"

"So we can't put them together. They'll need two bedrooms. I won't mind bunking with you Gracie. That way the girls can use my room," suggested Melinda, with a pleading look for understanding.

"Well, none of them can use mine," declared Libby, looking from Gracie to Melinda as if they had gone crazy.

"The boys can sleep in the guest room with me," Jeffrey said. He slipped behind his aunt to listen to the conversation. "If you'll round us up some quilts, Aunt Melinda, they can make a bed on the floor. We'll be fine," said Jeffrey, standing in the doorway. Deciding he had settled the problem, he squatted down in front of the children. "How about telling us who you are," he said..

The tallest girl pushed her stringy, long, brown hair away from her eyes, "My name's Amanda." She pointed to the small, brown haired boy taking his shoes off. "That's my brother, Bobby. You're not going to make us go out in that snowstorm are you? It's too far to our farm to walk in that." She spoke through trembling lips, puckering up to cry.

153

"Glad to meet you, Amanda. Don't you worry." said Jeffrey with a smile at her. He nodded at the little boy who was busy rubbing his red toes. "You're all staying here with us tonight. Who might you be?" Jeffrey asked the next girl. A plump, fair haired child, she was little shorter than Amanda.

"My name is Johnella," she said bashfully. Wiggling on the fireplace hearth, she twisted her hands together in her lap.

"And you little Miss Pigtails?" Jeffrey asked. He gave one of the little girl's brown pigtails a gentle tug.

"I'm Joyce," the small girl replied, flipping the pigtail back over her shoulder out of his reach.

"Well, that leaves you young man. What's your name?"

"Tommy," answered the red haired boy.

"It's nice to meet all of you," Melinda said, smiling warmly at each of them. "Now, Gracie, make yourself useful," she commanded. "Go make sure Miss Moxie told Aunt Pearlbee there will be five more for supper."

Gracie grumbled all the way to the kitchen about who died and left Melinda in charge all of a sudden. Maybe having those three girls wouldn't be so much bother. They seemed quiet enough, but those two boys looked devilishly ornery. They might be nothing but trouble. When she got back to the parlor, she should see if she could negotiate with Melinda and Moxie. If she said she didn't mind if the girls stayed the night, maybe she could get them to send those two boys on their way. Maybe Jeffrey could escort them across the street to the Bullocks. They were nice people. Sara was too kind hearted to turn anyone away during a snowstorm.

Pearlbee poured five cups of hot cocoa. "What's got a bee in yer bonnet, Miss Gracie?"

"You'll have five more mouths to feed for supper tonight. We thought you should know," grumbled Gracie,

154

staying by the door so she'd be able to make a fast get away if Pearlbee yelled.

"Ah's got the hot chocolate ready to take to them younguns. Little late notice if you ask me about fixin' more food fir supper though," grumped Pearlbee. "Supper will be late, but Ah's will fix extra food. Ah's was hopin' to head for home before it's too late."

"You can't do that. We need you to help watch these youngus," said Gracie, desperately.

"Thems not my younguns," retorted Pearlbee. She flinched when a scream that would rival any panther wailed through the mansion. "Mercy! What was that about?" Her eyes wide with fright, she waddle after Gracie, but she stayed back out of the way when she saw what caused the commotion.

At the base of the stairs, Libby, her hands covering her cheeks, breathed fast and hard like the air she sucked in each time would be her last. On the floor at her feet sat Bobby on the dragon painted in the middle of the large, red oriental rug. Middle ways up the oak stair railing perched Tommy. Frightened and slightly pale, both of the boys weren't moving a muscle. They stared at the wailing Libby.

"What happened here?" demanded Gracie, searching Libby's face for answers

"That boy hurled himself at me down the staircase as I started up. A few inches closer to me, and he'd have knocked me down as he slid by me," accused Libby, pointing at Bobby on the floor.

"Never did no such thing. I missed her by a mile," asserted Bobby, shaking his head vehemently in denial.

"Bobby, move over," called Tommy from his perch, waving his hand sideways. "You better back up, ladies. I want to see if I can shoot off here and sit on that dragon's head like

155

Bobby did." Before Gracie and Libby had time to scramble out of the way, he slid past them, sailed through the air and landed beside his friend.

Rolling her large, dark eyes toward the ceiling, Pearlbee muttered, "Lord, hep us that cain't help ourselves."

Weaving from side to side, Libby moaned like a devil possessed. Gracie grew certain that having those boys in the house was a decision Molly would regret when she came home. With her hands on her hips, Gracie marched over and stood in front of the boys just as Moxie, Melinda and Jeffrey burst into the dining room.

"That was fun," said Bobby, grinning a Tommy.

"Sure was," agreed Tommy, grinning back.

"Don't think you're going to try that again. You two are coming back into the parlor where we can watch you." Gracie grabbed each of them by an ear and pulled the squealing boys to their feet.

Melinda rushed in front of her. "Gracie don't do that. You're hurting the boys."

"Yeah, stop that you crazy old lady," squalled Tommy. When Gracie turned him loose, he balled his hands into fists, ready to fight.

Gracie grabbed Tommy by the shoulders and jerked him closer to her. "What did you say your name was?"

"I told you. Tommy," the boy spit out defiantly, wiggling in her grasp.

"Stand still. Your last name is --?" Gracie persisted.

"Brown."

A knowing look came over Gracie as she realized she knew this boy. "Melinda we're getting shut of this one. He's a ringer. That's one of Maudie Brown's ruffians. He lives right behind us. He can go home."

"I don't want to go out in this storm," whined the boy, looking from Moxie to Melinda for help.

"Miss Gracie, we can't take a chance he'll get lost. Me thinks, it's too late to send him out now," reasoned Moxie.

With more energy surging though her than she'd felt for awhile, Gracie grabbed Tommy by the arm and pulled him after her through the kitchen. She opened the back door, determined to get rid of Tommy. Snow swirled in with a blast of icy air, dusting her with a white frosting that glistened in the lamp light. She couldn't see past the gazebo. Realizing that Moxie was right about the storm being dangerous, Gracie turned loose of Tommy and shut the door. The boy slid behind Moxie for protection. He peeked out at Gracie. She glared at him and conceded, "Reckon we're stuck with him."

Pearlbee mumbled, "Ah knowed ah should have strung me a rope from here to home afore winter. Mercy, ah don't want to be stuck in this here crazy house tonight."

Tommy, standing with legs crossed, grabbed Moxie by the sleeve. He whispered, "Does this place have an indoor outhouse?"

"Yes indeed. It's called a water closet. Go up the stairs and down to the right to the end of the hall. It's the last door on your right," directed Moxie.

Both boys ran for the stairs. Gracie yelled after them, "You come right back down here when you're through. No nosing around up there by yourselves."

"All right," agreed Tommy, taking the stairs two at a time in a race to beat Bobby to the top.

With the boys out of sight, the women's turned their attention to the three cold girls in the parlor. Pearlbee hunted towels for Melinda and Moxie to rub the girls heads, drying their hair. Jeffrey sat down on the settee to watch. Libby went

157

back to reading.

Gracie couldn't sit still. She paced back and forth. She had the feeling felt she was the only one worrying about what mischief those rough boys could do upstairs by themselves. After she waited for what seemed like a sufficient time, she decided to go look for them. She stood outside the water closet and tried the door. It wouldn't open so she knocked and shouted, "Hey, you two die in there."

"No, but we can't get the door open. We want out of here," whimpered Bobby.

"Turn the door knob."

"We tried that. You turn the knob from your side, Miss Gracie," called Tommy.

Gracie turned the knob one way then the other. She pulled on it, tried shaking it and nothing happened. "I'll go get Mr. Jeffrey to help me. We'll get you out of there."

Gracie found Jeffrey in the kitchen, sampling a large kettle of chicken noodle soup simmering on the stove. "You need to come help me with those boys. They're locked in the water closet. They did something to the door. Now it won't open." Gracie paused. Her eyes lit up. "On second thought, think maybe we could leave them in there all night and worry about getting them out in the morning when we can send them home."

"We can't do that," responded Jeffrey with a glint of humor in his eyes.

"Why not?" Gracie demanded.

"We'll need to use that water closet ourselves," Jeffrey reasoned with a grin.

"Oh that's right," Gracie relented. "Guess you better hunt some tools and see if you can jimmy the lock."

158

Chapter 19

The next morning, the sun broke through the clouds. Brightness shimmered across the white caps on the hedge and trees. Shallow paths cut between deep drifts, making zig zag crevices down the street for travelers to use for paths.

Before they left for school, the children said their teacher told them to thank everyone for keeping them all night. Moser Mansion was again peaceful. Gracie listened to the quiet, but she didn't feel relief like she thought she would. One of her premonitions came over her. A warning that this might be the calm before another storm.

She was on her way down the entry hall to get a cup of coffee when she heard the knock on the door. "I'll get it," she offered as she past back by the parlor where everyone else was lazing after breakfast.

"Morning, Miss Gracie," greeted Sheriff Logan, touching his hat brim. "Quite a blizzard we had last night."

"Come on in out of the cold, Sheriff. It let us know winter is here. That's for sure. Must be something real important happening to get you out on a day like this when it's hard traveling. What brings you here?" asked Gracie as she shut the door behind him.

"I did some checking on Jeffrey Armstrong like you asked. I've come to take him down to the city jail for questioning. His story about coming from Missouri isn't true. The facts he knew came from the court house. The clerk told me a man matching Jeffrey's description was in there asking questions about Hiram Armstrong owning property in this county. Seems to me if Hiram was his father, Armstrong would already know what the man owns around here and his where abouts."

Grimly, Gracie remembered the premonition she had earlier that morning. "Mr. Jeffrey's in the parlor with Melinda and Miss Moxie. Come with me." Gracie led the way and stopped just inside the parlor door to point at Jeffrey. "That's him, Sheriff."

Sheriff Logan strode across the room and stood in front of Jeffrey. "You're under arrest Jeffrey Armstrong."

"Sir, I demand to know what is the meaning of this?" demanded Jeffrey. He lurched off the settee.

"This is terrible," gasped Melinda, wringing her hands together.

"Sheriff, sure and there has been some sort of horrible mistake," cried Moxie. "Jeffrey has done nothing wrong."

"This man has some explaining to do about missing property and some false statements he's made. I'm taking him in for questioning. Come along, Mr. Armstrong," the sheriff ordered.

"Miss Gracie, I expect this is your doing. Please tell the sheriff that he's making a mistake," Jeffrey said, looking at her pleadingly. Gracie looked away. All along, she had been trying to deal with the twinge of guilt she felt for asking the sheriff to look into this young man's life behind Melinda's back.

Melinda glared at her with a hurt look on her face as though Gracie had betrayed her. Gracie reasoned, "Now, Melinda, the sheriff has a job to do. We could all be in danger if this man is up to no good."

Moxie sobbed. Gracie turned to her. "Miss Moxie, I tried to tell all of you this man has been acting too sneaky to be honest. No one would listen to me. With Miss Molly away, I owe it to all of us to find out what Jeffrey Armstrong's hiding.

Whether, you admit it or not. Jeffrey hasn't been honest with us." Moxie looked away from her. Tears streamed down her face. Looking at those distraught faces, Gracie knew she could try to convince Melinda and Moxie all day long, but she could see she was only one with a level head at the moment.

Gracie walked over to Jeffrey. "So no, I won't say there's been a mistake. There's too many questions that you need to answer honestly. You best go on with the sheriff and straighten this out," Gracie said, standing her ground.

With a shake of his head, Jeffrey headed out the door with the sheriff right behind him. Moxie huddled on the settee, sobbing into her hanky.

Melinda whimpered, "How could you have my nephew arrested, Gracie?"

Gracie tried to defend herself. "I didn't have him arrested. That was the sheriff's idea not mine. You must admit, you don't know much about him. He never seems to have an answer that's good enough for the questions I asked him. Maybe he'll give Sheriff Logan the truth."

Through all the turmoil, Libby hugged her book to her and watched. Gracie turned to her. "Libby, tell Melinda it's for our protection. That man was living among us. The sheriff needs to get to the bottom of this. Find out what that young man's hiding."

Libby looked from Melinda wringing her hands to Moxie huddled on the settee, sobbing into her hanky. "Whatever you say, Gracie," she agreed weakly.

It was plain Libby wasn't about to take sides. She didn't want involved in this. Gracie turned back to Moxie and Melinda, desperate have them to understand. "I didn't have anything to do with that man getting arrested. I really didn't."

"If something happens to Mr. Jeffrey, I'll never forgive

161

ye," cried Moxie running from the room.

Melinda seared Gracie a hurt look and followed after Moxie. Gracie glanced at Libby. She had been watching intently. Quickly, she lowered her eyes and busied herself reading.

Gracie collapsed into her chair to think. In spite of all the suspicions she had about that young man, she kept picturing in her mind the look of betrayal in his eyes when he asked her to help him. Could she be wrong? Maybe she had misjudged him. Or maybe he was one of those deceiving folks that could sometimes look like a fox and then sometimes look like the thing the fox dragged in. Gracie didn't know if he was doing that or not. As bad as she hated to upset Melinda and Moxie, she couldn't back down yet. Let the sheriff see what answers he could come up with. If anyone could get that man to talk it would be Ben Logan.

The telephone rang several times. Finally, Gracie rose from her chair and walked out into the hall to answer it, hoping that whoever it was would hang up before she got there. "Hello."

"Hello, Miss Gracie. It's Molly. Hope I didn't interrupt something. It seemed to take awhile for you to answer. How are you?"

"You didn't interrupt anything. I'm fine." Gracie studied the gold plate tacked on the front of the telephone. It read National Electric Company. She didn't know what else to say. Finally, she came up with, "How are you and Mr. Orie?"

"Fine, too. I just called to let you all know we're coming in on the train tomorrow afternoon," continued Molly, eagerly.

"That's great news. We sure missed you, Miss Molly," said Gracie with as much sincerity as she could muster. All

162

sorts of ideas ran through her head about why Molly would not consider this a great homecoming once she found out what had been going on. With a dread she found hard to handle, Gracie figured she would be the one at the center of Molly's displeasure.

"Is everything all right there. You sound strange."

"Just glad you're coming home is all. See you tomorrow. Bye." Gracie dropped the receiver back into its cradle like it had suddenly gotten too hot to hold on to. She leaned her head on the wall and took a deep breath. It was better to hang up then let something slip to worry Molly. She'd find out what had been happening fast enough when she got home.

Sitting among the others at the silent table that night, Gracie felt as though she might as well be eating supper out in the yard. What difference did it make whether she froze to death outside in the snow or in the kitchen where all the cold shoulders were. The only words spoken came from her when she announced that Molly called. She and Mr. Orie were coming home tomorrow afternoon. Not one of the others at the table looked up to acknowledge that she spoke. She might as well have been talking to the pitcher pump in the sink.

Chapter 20

"Wait a minute, Maudie. I want to talk to you," called Gracie.

It seemed to Gracie that she'd heard the bang of the front door an awful lot that morning. An unusual run of people went in and out of the library. Finally, her curiosity got the better of her. Gracie peeked out the parlor door. Maudie Brown's back was to her, headed to the outside door.

"Wait a minute, Maudie. I want to talk to you," called Gracie.

The tall, thin lady turned around. "Morning, Gracie. Keeping warm enough?"

"Not too hard to do as long as I'm trapped in the parlor by the fire for the duration of the winter," grumped Gracie as she went to meet Maudie. "What are you doing here today?"

"I came to bring my book back. Miss Moxie sent word to me she's giving all the patrons back their dues. She's closing down the library. I sure hated to hear that," Maudie said regretfully.

"Maybe she'll open up again some day. Keep your ears open. You never know." Relief flushed through Gracie that Moxie was calling in the books she loaned out. Hopefully, she'd have ever last one of them back before Molly arrived that afternoon.

"That would be great if she does. By the way, thanks for taking care of my Tommy last night during the storm. I was right worried about him. It's good to know he'd been in where here, warm and safe. I best get home. Bye Gracie."

Gracie let out a long sigh. Evidently, Tommy hadn't elaborated about her objections to his spending the night. She

164

watched Maudie head for the door. She opened her mouth to invite the woman to sit with her in the parlor a spell but changed her mind. She'd have to be really desperate for company before she'd want to sit with Maudie, listening to all the antics of her brood.

After lunch, Melinda and Moxie walked down to the city jail to see Jeffrey. Libby was the only one left at home. "Libby, put down that book and come along with me to meet Miss Molly and Mr. Orie's train," said Gracie.

Hesitating, Libby said, "I'm not so sure that's a good idea."

"Now why ain't meeting Miss Molly's train not a good idea?" Boomed Gracie.

"I'm not so sure I want Melinda and Miss Moxie to catch me with you now that they are mad at you," snipped Libby.

"Those two aren't going to hold it against Libby you for going with me. The reason's to welcome Molly and Orie home. Miss Molly's feelings will be hurt if some of us don't meet the train," reasoned Gracie.

Thin, serious Libby walked beside Gracie, furtively watching around her. *She doesn't want to get caught with me if Melinda and Moxie happen to see us,* Gracie thought.. What a turn life had taken in the last few months. How had it happen that she began to tolerate snippy, Libby Hook to the point of not minding her company all for the sake of having a friend. She never thought she'd prefer Libby's company to none at all after so many years of living alone on the farm and not minding it. She reasoned her unexpected need for companionship must have rubbed off on her from all the time she'd spent with Melinda.

"Look at all the people scurrying around the depot,"

commented Gracie. Workers milled around cargo and sacks of mail on the brick platform.

"A sign the train is due soon when so many are preparing for it's arrival," replied Libby.

"Let's go in. We'll find out when the train will get here." Inside the depot, Gracie walked across the marble, tile floor with Libby staying close behind her. They bypassed a line of passengers waiting to buy tickets at one oak trimmed window and stopped at a window with the sign "Information" above it. The lady behind the window told Gracie that the train would arrive in just a few minutes.

"Let's wait outside. We can sit on one of those benches," suggested Libby, glancing around.. "To many strangers in here to suit me."

A row of benches lined the outside wall. Gracie sat down and leaned back against the light colored, stone wall that rose up to just above her head and changed to red brick. Next to her, Libby fiddled with the hanky in her hands while she stared at people passing by. Gracie grinned at the look on Libby's face. She studied each person up and down mistrustfully like she thought they might be up to no good.

In a few minutes, loud clanging reached the depot. Clamoring metal wheels ground on the rails. The bench the ladies sat on trembled. The black engine's gigantic smokestack, belched smoke and volumes of sparks. Looking out the window, the engineer's striped cap appeared then his head. He yanked on the warning whistle. Gracie and Libby put their hands over their ears to mute the deafening sound. The engine chugged by, leaving in its wake cinders and smoke floating in the air. The smoke fog drifted over the depot platform. Black specks of soot settle on Libby's dress. She vigorously brush her skirt. To her horror that action made things worse. Black streaks ran rampant over her dress. "This is the last time I wait for a train out here. Next time, I'm staying in the depot," she whined over the noise of the coaches rattling to a stop at the platform to let the passengers disembark.

"It was your idea to sit out here, but reckon you're right this time. My clothes are a mess, too," agreed Gracie. She didn't bother to brush her skirt off. Instead, she stretched her neck to look among the throng people climbing down the car steps. "Look, theres Miss Molly and Mr. Orie."

"See that traveling outfit she's wearing. Don't she look nice?" marveled Libby.

Molly came toward them in a black skirt with a red top, a fitted waist and large puff sleeves. A white lacy ascot ran from her neck down to the waist.

She spotted Gracie and Libby and waved. She turned to say something to Orie. Speeding up, she held onto her large, red hat. On top the hat, the red and white fluffy feathers fluffed up in the breeze, swaying as Molly hurried along the platform. "Oh, am I glad to see you two. I've missed you so." She gave Gracie a big hug.

For once, the older lady returned it. Gracie figured it might be the last time Molly liked her well enough to want to hug her. "Believe me, we missed you, too," Gracie stated adamantly.

Molly's eyebrows furrowed in worry at Gracie's so fervent out of character reply. Libby stepped around Gracie and distracted her. "Miss Molly, you look so nice in that outfit. It's a new one, isn't it?"

"Yes it is." Molly said, hugging Libby. "I have several new outfits I want to show all of you. I feel a little guilty about spending so much money on clothes in New York, but I couldn't help myself."

"Well, this is a fine howdy do. Isn't anyone going to tell me they missed me?" barked Orie, standing behind Molly.

"Of course, we missed you," stated Libby.

"Haven't had a decent glass of milk or a tasty vegetable since you left," replied Gracie with a serious look at Orie.

"Well, now I see how you are," Orie replied and laughed.

"Where is Miss Melinda and Moxie?" asked Molly, looking around the crowd. "I thought they'd come with you to meet us."

"They're down at the jail," said Gracie in a matter of fact tone.

"What are earth are they doing there?" gasped Molly, slapping her chest.

"Melinda's nephew has been arrested for being an imposture," offered Libby.

"And for stealing something of yours," shared Gracie.

"Golly Moses! This is awful. Poor Miss Melinda. She must be feeling so terrible," moaned Molly.

"What did he take?" asked Orie

"That ugly naked man statue in the hall which wouldn't have bothered me any if you hadn't set such store in it, Miss Molly," said Gracie, honestly.

"Oh no, this is horrible. Mr. Jeffrey didn't steal that statue," exclaimed Molly.

"How do you know he didn't? It's missing. We can't find it anywhere. He's the only stranger that's been in the house so stands to reason he took it," declared Gracie.

"It's not in the house. I had it taken to be refinished before we left on our honeymoon. The coating on it was pealing away. Oh dear, I feel as if this is all my fault. I just never thought to say anything to any of you with the excitement of the wedding." Molly looked as though she should take the blame for what had happened in her absence.

For a moment, Gracie thought she might let Molly do just that, but then her conscience nagged her. She couldn't do that to Molly. "Never mind that now. It ain't the only reason the sheriff wanted to question Jeffrey Armstrong. That young man has been sneaky acting. He's beat around the bush about everything we've asked him ever since he came. He's not who he says he is," declared Gracie. "The sheriff says he asked questions at the court house about Melinda's brother that he should have already known. It looked like Jeffrey was looking for the information so he'd be able to tell a convincing story to Melinda for reasons of his own."

"We better go down to the jail. At least we can tell the Sheriff that the man isn't a thief," said Orie to Molly.

"Not of that statue anyway," said Gracie, not wanting to relent.

169

Chapter 21

The walk to the small, brick jail was a short one. A good thing now that the sun was dipping down in the west. Cold air radiated off the snow piles, sending shivers through Gracie. She entered last behind the others, dreading to face Melinda and Moxie. It crossed Gracie's mind that the pot bellied stove would be the only warmth generated in that room when Melinda and Moxie realized she was among the group.

The two women looked mournfully like someone had died. They sat on ladder back chairs in front of one of the two cells. Jeffrey's face was wedged between the bars to be as close as he could Melinda and Moxie. They each held one of his outstretched hands. Perched with one hip on the desk, sheriff talked to Earl Bullock in his slow, western drawl. Leaned back in his chair with his arms folded behind his head, Earl listened. His feet were propped on his desk.

"Hey, looks who's back from their honeymoon," boomed the sheriff. He stood up when he heard stomping feet as the group tried to dislodge the snow stuck to their shoes. "Welcome back, folks."

"Hello, Orie and Miss Molly. Sorry you had to come back to such goings on," admitted Earl, taking his feet off the desk.

"Hi, Earl. What you doing behind that desk?" Orie asked, sounding surprised.

"I'm the town marshal now," Earl said.

"Congratulations, Earl." Orie rushed forward to shake the man's hand. "You couldn't have picked a better or fairer man for the job, Sheriff."

Molly walked over to the cell. She patted Melinda's shoulder. The little lady gave Molly a weak smile through tears. The moment she saw Gracie, she wrinkled her nose in a snarled at her. Moxie jumped up. Unable to speak, she hugged Molly.

Molly turned to the sheriff. "We had to stop by on our way home. We wanted to let you know right away that Jeffrey didn't steal my statue. I had it shipped off to get a new coating put on it. It should be back any time now."

Sheriff Logan gave Gracie a quizzical look. "Well, I'll be. Miss Gracie was so sure he took it," he said, scratching his head.

Molly gave Gracie a questioning glance. She ducked her head to avoid Molly's gaze.

Jeffrey gripped the bars. He said to the sheriff, "See I'm innocent just like I said. Let me out of here."

Sheriff Logan walked over to the cell. "Not so fast young man. You have some explaining to do. You might as well start telling us the truth. You're not going to be let out of jail so you can go back to deceiving these two ladies." He patted Melinda's shoulder. "I have to warn you to be careful what you say. I've done some investigating down in Missouri where you say you came from. We know that Hiram Armstrong had three girls and no sons. Now what do you say to that?"

Jeffrey avoided the hurt look on Melinda's face. He said in his defense, "I really am her nephew."

Gracie edged closer to the cell. "He sure is a stubborn cuss," she stated out of the corner of her mouth to Molly. She faced the man behind the bars. "If you're who you say and honest about your dealings, then why have you been inspecting everyone you meet as if they might know something that could do you harm?"

"I can explain that if I have to, but I wish you'd just believe I am Aunt Melinda's nephew," the young man implored, gripping the cell bars tight enough to cause white knuckles.

"You're still trying to tell us that Hiram Armstrong is your father even though he never had a son?" Sheriff Logan asked.

"No, that's not it," said Jeffrey, looking distraught. He said to Melinda, "I let you believe that lie. I am sorry for that."

"How can it be you are my nephew then?" asked Melinda, painfully bewildered.

"My mother was Lorena Armstrong," blurted out Jeffrey.

"I never knew she married," said Melinda with a baffled expression.

"She didn't. That's why she never wanted you to find out about me. The fact is, I wanted to get to know you so bad I decided to tell you that I was Hiram's son so you'd like me right off. From what the lady who raised me said Mother told her, you might not want anything to do with me if I said I was Lorena's son. Mother had told her you hated her," accused Jeffrey.

"That's nonsense! I loved your mother, and I'd love you no matter if you were Hiram's son or Lorena's," declared Melinda. Jumping to her feet, she faced Jeffrey.

"That's not what my mother thought." Jeffrey gave her the saddest look Gracie thought she'd ever seen. Differently, the man was what the fox dragged in at the moment.

"Your mother was mistaken. This has been a terrible misunderstanding. Please, Sheriff, let my nephew out of that cell. He doesn't belong here," pleaded Melinda.

"I reckon you're right ma'am. Sorry about the mistake

over the statue, young feller." Sheriff Logan reached for one of keys on the wooden peg and unlocked the cell door.

"That's all right, Sheriff. You're just protecting my aunt. I can appreciate that I looked suspicious."

"Wait a minute," demanded Gracie. "Who have you been watching out for all the time you've been here, young man? You didn't answer me before. I've been afraid you did something wrong that would put us all in danger."

"You don't miss much, Miss Gracie," said Jeffrey, giving her a wry grin. "I kept hoping I'd see some man who looked like he could be my father. Hoping Aunt Melinda might see someone and let something slip about him being a friend of her sister years ago. Along with the hope of finding out who my father was, I feared if I did find my father, he'd give my secret away to Aunt Melinda about who my mother was. I thought when she found out, she wouldn't want anything to do with me. I've come to love her like a mother. I didn't want to lose that." Jeffrey put his arms around Melinda and gave her a hug.

"Well, there you are, Miss Gracie. Now let's go home," suggested Molly. "I want to find out what's happened since we left, and Miss Melinda and Mr. Jeffrey need to have time to catch up for real this time."

173

Chapter 22

Molly ushered the group back to Moser Mansion. She stopped them in the entry hall. "Miss Melinda why don't you take Mr. Jeffrey in the library to talk in private. The rest of us can settle down in the parlor in front of the fire. Orie and I can catch up on what's been happening around here while we warm up."

"No, you might as well all hear my story about Lorena if you want," said Melinda. She looked at Jeffrey for his approval. "If it's all right with Jeffrey, that is?"

"Of course it is. After all, you consider these people your family," agreed Jeffrey.

Molly ushered them all into the parlor. "All right then, sit down. We'll listen to Miss Melinda's story."

Melinda collapsed beside Jeffrey and Moxie on the settee. "Really there's not much to tell," she began softly, looking at her clasped hands in her lap. "Lorena was such a pretty girl. She attracted the beaus so much easier than I could. Quite frankly, I was jealous of her. We tended to compete for the same gentlemen callers and argued way too much over trivial things. I suppose it was sibling rivalry to start with, but by the time of Hiram's wedding, we couldn't speak civilly at all to each other. Lorena looked so pretty the day of the wedding. I felt like her dress was nicer than mine. Her hair was never out of place while my hair was always a mess of curls heaped on my head or flying all over. I felt so mousy when I compared myself to her." Melinda paused. She sat silently, her face reflected a melancholic scene from the past.

"Well, what happened?" barked Gracie, leaning forward in her chair to hear every word.

Startled back to reality by the sound of Gracie's voice, Melinda patted Jeffrey's knee. "I'm so sorry for my part in your mother's unhappiness. I never thought she'd take to heart what I said and disappear like she did."

Leaning around Jeffrey to look at Melinda, Moxie asked, "What did ye say that was so terrible, Miss Melinda? I can't imagine ye being mean to anyone."

Melinda scrunched up her nose and gritted out the words. "We were the bridesmaids for Hiram's wedding. Standing behind Lorena during the ceremony, I turned green with envy watching my pretty sister. With no thought at all about what I was about to do, I tapped her on the shoulder. When she turned her head, I whispered nastily in Lorena's ear that I wished I had her pretty hair, and she had a wart on the end of her nose. She looked so hurt. Right away I wished I could take back my thoughtless, hurtful remark, but without saying a word, Lorena turned her back to me. I looked for her later at the reception to say I was sorry, but she had left. Later I found out she had left Locked Rock. I never saw her again. I've felt the burden of guilt ever since for driving my sister away." She buried her face in a handkerchief and cried.

"Try not to take the blame for what happened entirely on yourself, Aunt Melinda. From what the lady who raised me said, Mother knew she was pregnant when she left Locked Rock. She was scared and confused. She didn't want to bring shame on her family. I suspect she especially didn't want you to know how she had misbehaved. She felt that the family would always hold it against her. So you see she was hiding from all the family not just you. She never intended to come back to Locked Rock even if you'd had the chance to beg her."

Melinda took the hanky away from her face. "Why didn't she just marry your father?"

"I was told that wasn't possible. He was a married man."

"Do you know who he was?" asked Gracie. "Maybe he still lives in Locked Rock."

"No, Mother took that information to her grave. I just have what little details my mother told the woman who raised me. He was an important man of means. I looked through a book in the library on the history of Locked Rock, but no one in the book seemed to fit.

"So that's why you took that book. I saw you take it. I wondered why you were so secretive about borrowing it," said Gracie.

"That's why," Jeffrey answered. He turned back to his aunt. "Can you tell me what man my mother was friendly with before she left town?"

"Several young men including my late husband which I must confess was another reason I was upset with Lorena. None of those men were married. Our parents would never have permitted that kind of behavior to continue if they knew about it. Lorena was right about that." Melinda paused to think a minute. "Oh dear, it's been so long ago. I need to have some time to think about this."

"Of course, you do. Take your time. If you don't mind now that all this is out in the open, I'd like to stick around for awhile and really get to know you," offered Jeffrey, hopefully.

Melinda smiled at him through tears. "I don't mind at all."

"Neither do I," said Moxie, grinning at him.

"Now let's hear what else happened while we were gone," said Molly.

176

"Best let Miss Moxie start first." Gracie nodded at Moxie to let her know it was time to confess.

That began the tale of how Moxie tried to start Locked Rock's first library so she could have a job. Molly grimaced at the mention of checking out her first additions, but Moxie quickly explained that there was no harm done. She had gotten them all back, and they were in good shape.

Molly gave a sigh of relief. "So what are the plans for the library then?"

The library is going to be built thanks to some funding and matching money from the town people, but we don't have enough money to buy books, too."

"How about all those old books that Gracie's rocker was buried under in the attic," suggested Libby. "You said you wanted to clean up the attic, Molly."

"That's a wonderful idea, Libby. Moxie feel free to help yourself to all those books as a start to the new library," offered Molly.

"Thank you, Molly. That's great news," exclaimed Moxie, clapping her hands together.

"Now did anything else happen while we was gone?" Molly looked from one to the other of the ladies with an uncertain look on her face.

Melinda told about the Halloween party at the Bullocks house, and how they were so worked up when they came home that finding Jeffrey on the settee scared all of them. Since then he had been staying in the spare bedroom so she hoped that Molly didn't mind.

"Of course, I don't mind. We haven't a use for that room at the moment and soon as Jeffrey gets on his feet, I'm sure he'll find a place of his own," Molly said as if hoping her meaning would be clear. She didn't want him to become a permanent house guest. "Won't you, Jeffrey?"

"Of course, I will Miss Molly. Thank you for your hospitality," he affirmed gratefully.

"Does this mean I'm out of the dog house with everyone now that this whole mess has turned out all right?" asked Gracie, looking sheepishly at the oriental rug under her feet.

"Of course, I can't stay mad at you for long, Gracie. I know you were just looking out for my welfare," offered Melinda, patting Gracie's hand.

"Me thinks, we need to forget the whole thing and just start over," suggested Moxie.

"Well, now that about does it for news around here I expect. We should get ready to go eat supper soon. I need to change out of this traveling dress first." Molly started to get up.

"Hold on one minute. We aren't done yet," declared Gracie, straightening up in her chair and throwing back her shoulders. "We haven't told you about the blizzard. We had to take care of them school kids cause you offered."

"It snowed while we were gone, and the children came here. Wonderful! Oh, I'm so sorry I missed that. That must have been fun."

Gracie vigorously shook her head no.

"Oh, it wasn't wonderful," relented Molly, slowly shaking her head in imitation of Gracie..

"No, it was a nightmare if you ask me," grumped Gracie.

"Now, Gracie, it wasn't as bad as all that. Jeffrey broke the knob on the water closet door to rescue the boys," said Melinda.

"The knob on the water closet is broke," repeated Molly, grimacing.

"The boys liked to knocked Libby down on the stairs when they came flying down the railing," stated Gracie.

"Oh dear," gasped Molly, looking a Libby who took on the look of a victim.

"But Moxie did a fine job of settling the children down," complimented Melinda.

"Why thank ye, Miss Melinda."

"All I got to say is, don't you ever leave us alone again during the winter if it's going to snow," declared Gracie, jabbing her finger at Molly. "You'll find out right enough what happens when those ruffians invade us."

"All right, Gracie, you have a deal. I plan to stay home during the winter from now on," agreed Molly. "Well it seems like you have had lots of excitement while we were gone. It does look like you have all managed to come out of the experience no worse for wear." Then she hid her mouth behind her hand, trying to stifle a giggle for fear she'd upset Gracie more.

A few days later, Gracie sat down for the Thanksgiving dinner in the fancy dining room with the others at Moser mansion. It was a relief to feel a good feeling spreading through her after so many bad premonitions. She felt a new beginning was a foot as she looked around the table. A good feeling this time after having so many bad premonition Melinda and Moxie had Jeffrey seated between them where they could both bid for his attention. Moxie glowed up at him each time he spoke to her. Melinda smiled with the pride of a new mother looking at her offspring. Quiet for once, Libby seemed more peaceful than she had in days. For her sake, Gracie hoped she was resigned to the fact that this was her family. Orie and Molly looked at each other and smiled often, content now that they had settled down to a daily routine together.

The bowls of food had just started around the table when there was a knock on the front door.

"Who could that be?" Molly asked, looking at Orie.

Her husband shrugged his shoulders. "I don't know, but I'll go find out."

"Whoever it is, ask them to stay for supper. We have plenty," Molly called after Orie.

"Hello there, Millard. Come on in out of the cold," greeted Orie loud enough that he could be heard down the hall to the dining room.

"Thought as long as I was in town, I'd check to see if you'd made it home yet," Millard replied.

At the sound of the familiar, deep voice, Gracie crunched down in her chair. She had the feeling her premonitions of impending danger had gone haywire this time. She had just had thoughts that this night would be a good one. Goes to show she couldn't guess right every time.

Smiling impishly at Gracie's reaction, Melinda nudged her hand to get Gracie to accept the corn bowl. Gracie frowned at Melinda and snatched the bowl out of her hands. She kept her ear turned toward the hall to listen.

Orie said, "I was coming out in the morning to let you know I'm back. I hoped the roads would be passable by then so I could get out there. I wanted to let you know you can stop doing my chores. I sure do appreciate the help. Thank you so much. Come on in and eat Thanksgiving dinner with us. We just started and there's plenty of food.

Gracie felt ill at the thought of sitting at the same table with Millard Sokal. Her chest tightened like she didn't have the energy to inhale a decent breath of air. She strained to hear the old farmer's answer. At the same time, she wondered what

180

would work as an excuse to get her out of there. She could honestly say she was too sick to eat and go to her room.

But she didn't have to do that. She heard Millard say no. Orie thanked him again for his help and closed the door.

Suddenly, it wasn't relief Gracie felt but disappointment and anger. Hadn't Millard told her at the dance he would be talking to her again. Well, he had his chance, and he left without coming in to even say hello. Just like a man to say one thing and do another. Never could trust the lot of them as far as she could throw them.

"Gracie, take the bread. Did you hear me?" Melinda asked, shaking a platter heaped with homemade bread at her arm.

"What? Oh sure, I heard you," insisted Gracie. She hoped Melinda didn't interpret the look on her face. Melinda might just decide to tell Molly about Millard and her past. One thing might lead to another. Melinda would tell all about their chance meeting as the wedding barn dance.

For once Melinda understood Gracie's uncomfortableness. She patted her friend on the arm and said softly, "If you heard me, will you take the bread platter, please?"

"Sure I will," Gracie said sheepishly.

The meal was about over when Moxie drew everyone's attention. "Sure and it is, I have an announcement to make everyone."

"Oh how wonderful," gushed Melinda, looking from Moxie to Jeffrey.

Blushing, Moxie looked at Jeffrey's puzzled expression and realized why Melinda was so excited. "Now wait a wee moment until I tell ye, Miss Melinda. What I wanted to say was, I have a new job. I hope ye all approve."

181

"Here we go again," said Gracie, rolling her eyes toward the ceiling.

"That's great news. What's the job?" Asked Molly, giving Gracie a stern look to silence her.

"I'm the society editor for the Locked Rock Review. My first assignment has already been printed in the newspaper. Wait til ye see it." Moxie took off for the library and came back flipping the pages to the society section. "Here tis, Molly."

Molly glanced at the article and laughed.

"What does it say?" Asked Orie.

Molly read, "The title is "Wedding of Orie and Molly Lang held on October 20, 1903." She glanced at her husband. "It appears to be a write up on our wedding, Orie. Looks like you and I have made society news in the Locked Rock Review, dear husband."

Gracie leaned over and whispered to Melinda, "I think I should warn you, to be very careful what you say. This job of Miss Moxie's might not be a good thing around you."

"Why on earth not? I think it's wonderful Miss Moxie has a job," retorted Melinda under her breath.

"No offense, but I know how you like to talk. It's more important that ever that you watch what you say around that girl. Otherwise you mark my words, you'll find yourself quoted in the newspaper for the whole county to read," warned Gracie.

At first, Melinda was angered by Gracie's insinuation that she was a blabber mouth. Suddenly, she realized what Gracie was so afraid would come out for all to read. "Father inn Heaven, you've nothing to fear. Stories abut the men in your life are for you and only you to tell."

Gracie whispered, "Not men. Just one man."

"Eat your supper, Gracie," rasped Melinda. She noted the questioning looks from Jeffrey and Moxie. She met them with a smile and a purely innocent look. She wasn't about to let Gracie upset her on Thanksgiving especially this one with all the people she loved around her.

Gracie finally calmed down when she realized Melinda meant to keep her secret. Gratification swept over her at what a good friend Melinda was to put up with her crude ways.

Reckon Melinda has the right idea. She studied each person at the table. Being alone on the farm wasn't really what she always thought it was cracked up to be. Living in Moser Mansion with these nice folks was much better.

Fay Risner lives with her husband, Harold, on a central Iowa acreage along with their sheep, milk goats, chickens, rabbits, cats and a dog. They have one son, Duane. She divides her time between writing, working at the Keystone Nursing Care Center, enjoying country life, gardening and fishing. She has sold five stories to Good Old Days magazine and entered numerous short story and essay contests, placing twenty nine times. For more information about her life and interests as well as her accomplishments visit her website at http://www.booksbyfay@tripod.com

If you liked this book try others in this series.

Neighbor Watchers
Chance Of A Sparrow
County Seat Killer
Moser Mansion's Ghosts

Plus others
The Dark Wind Howls Over Mary
My Children Are More Precious Than Gold
Ella Mayfield's Pawpaw Militia
Butterfly And Angel Wings
A Teapot, Ghosts, Bats & More
Open A Window
Hello Alzheimer's Good Bye Dad
Western Shorts

All can be purchased on Amazon.com

3476720